Dear Reader,

Welcome to the world of Silhouette Desire, where you can indulge yourself every month with romances that can only be described as passionate, powerful and provocative!

The always fabulous Elizabeth Bevarly offers you May's MAN OF THE MONTH, so get ready for *The Temptation of Rory Monahan.* Enjoy reading about a gorgeous professor who falls for a librarian busy reading up on how to catch a man!

The tantalizing Desire miniseries TEXAS CATTLEMAN'S CLUB: LONE STAR JEWELS concludes with *Tycoon Warrior* by Sheri WhiteFeather. A Native American ex-military man reunites with his estranged wife on a secret mission that renews their love.

Popular Peggy Moreland returns to Desire with a romance about a plain-Jane secretary who is in love with her *Millionaire Boss.* The hero-focused miniseries BACHELOR BATTALION by Maureen Child continues with *Prince Charming in Dress Blues,* who's snowbound in a cabin with an unmarried woman about to give birth! *Baby at His Door* by Katherine Garbera features a small-town sheriff, a beautiful stranger and the bundle of love who unites them. And Sara Orwig writes a lovely tale about a couple entering a marriage of convenience in *Cowboy's Secret Child.*

This month, Silhouette is proud to announce we've joined the national campaign "Get Caught Reading" in order to promote reading in the United States. So set a good example, and get caught reading all six of these exhilarating Desire titles!

Enjoy!

Joan Marlow Golan

Joan Marlow Golan
Senior Editor, Silhouette Desire

Please address questions and book requests to:
Silhouette Reader Service
U.S.: 3010 Walden Ave., P.O. Box 1325, Buffalo, NY 14269
Canadian: P.O. Box 609, Fort Erie, Ont. L2A 5X3

Tycoon Warrior
SHERI WHITEFEATHER

Published by Silhouette Books
America's Publisher of Contemporary Romance

Special thanks and acknowledgment are given
to Sheri WhiteFeather for her contribution
to the TEXAS CATTLEMAN'S CLUB: LONE STAR JEWELS series.

This book is dedicated to my Texas Cattleman's Club sisters, Jennifer Greene,
Sara Orwig, Cindy Gerard and Kristi Gold. I hope we can do it again sometime.

Special thanks to Lee Bundy for being my mom and my personal assistant,
Joan Marlow Golan and Karen Kosztolnyik for inviting me
to do this series, TSgt. Gerard Howard for answering questions
about the United States Air Force, and Harold (Little Bull) Hull, Jr.
for putting me in touch with a former Navy SEAL.
Here's to secret Apaches and telephone conversations
that never existed.

SILHOUETTE BOOKS

RECYCLED PAPER

ISBN 0-373-76364-6

TYCOON WARRIOR

Copyright © 2001 by Harlequin Books S.A.

Books by Sheri WhiteFeather

Silhouette Desire

Warrior's Baby #1248
Skyler Hawk: Lone Brave #1272
Jesse Hawk: Brave Father #1278
Cheyenne Dad #1300
Night Wind's Woman #1332
Tycoon Warrior #1364

SHERI WHITEFEATHER

lives in Southern California and enjoys ethnic dining, summer powwows and visiting art galleries and vintage clothing stores near the beach. Since her one true passion is writing, she is thrilled to be a part of the Silhouette Desire line. When she isn't writing, she often reads until the wee hours of the morning.

Sheri also works as a leather artisan with her Muscogee Creek husband. They have one son and a menagerie of pets, including a pampered English bulldog and four equally spoiled Bengal cats. She would love to hear from her readers. You may write to her at: P.O. Box 5130, Orange, California 92863-5130.

"What's Happening in Royal?"

NEWS FLASH, May—Everyone in the town of Royal is talking about a possible reconciliation of our favorite marrieds—Dakota and Kathy Lewis! 'Course, all those single gals are hoping it isn't true, as the swoon-inspiring former air force lieutenant Dakota Lewis proves a mighty catch. But this hunk's Comanche heart appears destined to belong to his beautiful wife, Kathy....

Seems the reunion began when woman-of-the-world Kathy returned to Royal unexpectedly to meet with our dashing Texas Cattlemen—her hubby, Dakota, included—behind closed doors. And where-oh-where did Kathy and Dakota disappear to soon after?

Perhaps our boys at the Cattleman's Club can finally give us some answers? We're waiting here with bated breath.... Stay tuned!

One

Retired air force lieutenant Dakota Lewis sat upright in a leather recliner, studying his home. Would the ranch look the same to Kathy?

Of course it would, he told himself a second later. He hadn't changed a thing. Not one cowboy novelty, not one Indian artifact. She would recognize every cow skull, every antler, every ceremonial pipe.

An ensemble of cedar, pine and mahogany made up Dakota's living room. He hadn't chosen pieces that belonged in sets. He preferred eclectic furnishings—hacienda-style trunks, tables topped with clay-colored tiles, mirrors framed in tooled leather.

He turned his attention back to his guests. They weren't discussing the mission at this point. Someone had made a reference to his wife. Was it Aaron Black? Sheikh Ben Rassad? Dr. Justin Webb? It wasn't Matthew Walker because Matt wasn't married.

No, but he was engaged. Happily engaged.

Hell, Dakota thought. What was wrong with him? The other men in the room were his friends, his peers. He had no right to envy them. They were all members of the Texas Cattleman's Club, the most exclusive gentlemen's club in the state. They were all wealthy—filthy rich, some might say. And they were all either happily married or happily engaged.

All except himself.

Dakota's estranged wife was due to arrive at his ranch any minute. Kathy had left three years before, a choice she hadn't even bothered to explain. Dakota had come home from an assignment to find her gone—her side of the closet empty, the scented lotions she favored no longer lined up on the bathroom counter. Two years of marriage shot to hell, and Dakota didn't know why. He had loved his wife, was certain she had loved him, too. Yet she'd walked out on him, saddling him with an emotional wound festering deep in his gut.

A wound that had become exceptionally active today. The top-secret mission the Cattleman's Club's members had come to discuss involved Kathy. She was the Foreign Service consular being teamed with Dakota. Together they would fly to Asterland, a small European country on the brink of a revolution.

The doorbell rang. Dakota excused himself from the other men and strode toward the entryway. Checking his watch, he tightened his jaw. Thirteen hundred hours. She was right on time.

Kathy stood on the other side of the door, slim and elegant, her thick, hard-to-hold hair coiled in a neat chignon. She wore a beige pantsuit and an emerald blouse that intensified the color of her eyes. Cat's eyes, he'd always called them. Exotic eyes and fire-tinted hair, features that belied Kathy's proper nature.

Neither spoke. Instead their gazes locked, and they stared at each other for what seemed like the longest moment of Dakota's life.

"It's good to see you," she said finally, extending her hand.

Polite pleasantries, he thought. What else could he do? This was business, and Dakota viewed his work as the number-one priority in his life. He wouldn't let anything stand in the way of an assignment, not even the pain shooting from his gut to his heart.

"It's good to see you, too," he responded, clasping her hand as though her touch wouldn't affect him. It did, of course. Her hand felt small and feminine, her skin soft and warm against his own.

He invited her in, cursing the memories threatening to surface. Her fragrance drifted to his nostrils like fresh strawberries smothered in cream. Kathy preferred scented lotions to heavy perfumes, aromas that never failed to make Dakota hungry.

Suddenly he fought the temptation to uncoil her hair, let it fall across her shoulders. He hadn't forgotten the woman he loved, hadn't forgotten how she looked soaking in the tub, her fiery tendrils slipping free from the pins that secured them, her long, sleek body creamy and smooth.

How many times had he watched her slide a washcloth down her arms and over her breasts? And how many times had he carried her, soaking wet, to their bed?

"Dakota? Are the others here?"

Kathy's question jarred him back to reality. Damn it. He stood in the tiled entryway, his hormones battling for control. How in the hell had he let that happen?

"Yes, they're here." He escorted his estranged wife to the living room, hating himself for the moment of weakness.

Like the Texas gentlemen they were, the other men rose as Kathy entered the room. Aaron Black came forward to hug her. How easily Kathy embraced Aaron, Dakota thought, wondering why a fist of rivalry gripped him hard and quick. Not only was Aaron blissfully married with a baby on the way, he was also a good friend, the American diplomat who had introduced Dakota to Kathy nearly six years before.

Kathy shook hands with the others, and soon they settled into their seats.

As Kathy crossed her legs, Dakota poured her a ginger ale from the wet bar. He didn't stop to ask her preference. He knew what Kathy's favorite soft drink was, and he still stocked the bar with it.

She thanked him quietly, the ice in her glass crackling. He poured himself a cola, opting to keep his hands busy. The urge to loosen her hair had returned.

How different they were, he thought, how opposite. Kathy was renowned for her grace and diplomacy, whereas Dakota was as rough-hewn as his taste in furniture, often solving matters with force.

Lifting his cola from the bar, Dakota took a swig, wondering if he should have spiked it with rum—something, anything to take the edge off. How could a woman skilled in conversation walk out on her husband without the slightest explanation? How could she ignore what they had meant to each other? The love? The passion?

Dakota didn't need to ask Kathy where she had been for the past three years. He already knew. She had gone to Washington, D.C., to serve in the Bureau of Consular Affairs, leasing a spacious apartment in an exclusive suburb and furnishing it with antiques. Prior to that, she had been on an extended leave of absence, debating whether to end her career. For Kathy, living abroad in the Foreign Service had become stressful. She wanted to remain in Texas. Or so she'd said.

Regardless, locating her in Washington had been easy. Keeping his distance had been the tough part. But Dakota figured Kathy didn't want to be confronted, didn't want him standing on her doorstep, demanding to know why she had left. So consequently, Dakota's pride—his hard-baked masculine ego—had managed to keep him at bay.

Sheikh Rassad drew Kathy into the meeting, pulling Dakota in as well.

"Are you familiar with the events leading up to this mission?" Ben asked her. "Are there any details that are not clear?"

"Aaron briefed me," she responded. "I know the Lone Star jewels were stolen. And I'm also aware that they've been recovered." She sat with her usual graceful posture, giving the sheikh her undivided attention. "Albert Payune, the Grand

Minister of Asterland, masterminded the robbery, intending to use the jewels to fund a revolution. Which is where Dakota and I come in. It's our job to make sure that revolution doesn't happen.''

The sheikh leaned forward. ''Aaron informed us that you are well acquainted with the king and queen.''

''That's true. I'm very fond of the royal family, and I don't intend to see them lose their country.'' She placed her glass on a coaster, sending the sheikh a reassuring smile. ''I've already made arrangements for Dakota to accompany me to Asterland for the queen's birthday ball. And since he will be visiting as my guest, his presence won't arouse suspicion.''

Dakota listened, although he had already been briefed by Aaron. The plan had been carefully orchestrated. Dakota's initial arrival in Asterland must appear to be of a personal nature. And what could be more personal than traveling with his wife? They wouldn't need to fake their cover, at least not on paper. They would be playing themselves.

Almost.

They would have to pretend to be in the midst of a reconciliation, a couple mending their marriage.

Dakota glanced at Kathy, and she barely returned his gaze. She appeared poised and professional, but he could sense her uneasiness. The same uneasiness that swept through him.

How were they going to pull this off if they couldn't look at each other? Couldn't relax in each other's presence? Dakota glanced at Kathy again, his chest constricting with a familiar ache. Somehow, someway, they would have to. The future of a country was at stake. And this mission was far too risky for mistakes.

Kathy exhaled a quiet breath. When Aaron asked Dakota a question, he shifted his attention, giving her the opportunity to study him.

The years had been good to Dakota Lewis, aging him in a way that made him even more handsome, more rugged. He was half Comanche and half Texan—a tall, solid man with eyes that changed from brown to black, depending on his mood. His profile presented a determined jaw and high, slanted cheekbones. Everything about him boasted masculinity. His midnight hair, although short by most standards, was slightly longer than the military style he had worn while on active duty.

Active duty? Aside from allowing his hair to grow, retirement hadn't changed Dakota Lewis. He'd gone from Special Forces assignments to privately funded missions without a hitch in his long, powerful stride. Danger flowed through his veins like liquid; it was his life force, his blood. Kathy considered men like Dakota adrenaline junkies—men who would never give up the fight, the need to save the world.

Of course, adrenaline junkies didn't settle down with their wives. Instead they left them behind, left them alone to wait and wonder, praying frantically for their husbands' safe return.

How many assignments had he been on since she'd left? Did he miss her the way she had missed him? Or had his work filled the void? Dakota had loved her—that much she knew. Only he hadn't loved her the way she'd needed. Dakota's work had always come first. Kathy couldn't bear being second-best in her husband's heart.

And then when she'd lost the baby—

Her breath hitched. Oh, God. Don't think about the baby. Not here, not now. She placed a hand over her stomach. When would the pain go away, the ache of losing Dakota's child? How many years would have to pass? How many years before she stopped wishing every dark-haired toddler she saw was hers?

Dakota turned toward her, and she removed her hand from her stomach. Kathy had learned long ago how to keep her emotions in check, and she wouldn't give herself away now. Dakota didn't know about the baby. He had been in the Middle East tracking gunrunners when she'd miscarried—alone and afraid, missing her husband and crying for the baby they would never hold. A child she had wanted desperately.

"How well do you know Albert Payune?" Sheikh Rassad asked, catching Kathy off guard.

She lifted her chin and concentrated on the mission, the reason she had agreed to fly to Asterland with Dakota.

"I know Payune well enough to form an opinion of him," she responded. The sheikh's interest in Payune didn't surprise her, nor did his active participation in this meeting. She knew the sheikh's new bride had been formerly promised to Albert Payune in an arranged marriage. "Payune is a clever man, but he's arrogant, too. Much too vain to be considered charming. He isn't likable, but he knows how to command attention. He prides himself on power. Craves it, one could say."

"The perfect profile of a revolutionist," Aaron added. "It's quite possible Payune's sanity borders on his desire to succeed."

Matthew Walker joined in the conversation, mentioning his fiancée—Lady Helena of Asterland, a cousin to the royal family—a lady who shared Kathy's opinion of Payune.

Only Dakota and Dr. Webb remained silent. The doctor sat patiently, but Dakota rose from his chair and crossed the room, heading toward the cowhide-covered bar.

Kathy watched him. He moved like a long, fluid animal stalking his prey. It was the Comanche in him, she thought. The warrior preparing to count coup, his mental focus merging with his physical being. She recognized the look, the walk, the adrenaline charge that took him into the next battle, the next mission. This would be the man going after Albert Payune.

Had Dakota acquired another scar since she'd seen him last? Another mark of valor?

Kathy knew every inch of his body, every taut muscle, every hard ridge and flat plane. She also knew his hands were mildly callused, capable of inflicting pain or pleasure, depending on his objective. She had always been on the receiving end of pleasure, those large callused hands surprisingly gentle against her flesh. Dakota Lewis was as skilled a lover as he was a warrior.

Don't think about that now, she told herself. Focus on the mission. The reason she had agreed to help the Cattleman's Club.

When the meeting ended, the other men departed, leaving Dakota and Kathy alone. She clutched her handbag and stood. Suddenly the smell of wood and leather made her homesick. The ranch looked the same, the living room cluttered with rustic charm. Pillows, lamps, paintings, bronze statues—every piece told a Western story.

Was the bedroom the same? Had he kept the items she had chosen? The canopy bed, the hand-painted dresser, the horse weather vane sitting atop a Chippendale desk? The ranch belonged to Dakota, a custom-built home he had helped design ten years before. But when Kathy had married him, he'd asked her to redecorate the bedroom—fill it with her flair, her flavor. So she had combined formal antiques with Western relics, candles with cowboy boots, Waterford crystal with carved wood. The end result had pleased Dakota, especially the massive bed.

A bed Kathy had no right to remember. She didn't belong in this house. Loving Dakota didn't mean she could live with him, wait months on end for him to return from the missions that consumed him.

How ironic that they would come together for an assignment, for one of the secret operations engineered by the Texas Cattleman's Club. The members of that prestigious club weren't just established businessmen. They were Lone Star warriors, men who vowed to serve and protect.

Only Dakota hadn't protected her. He hadn't been there when she'd lost the baby.

"I think we should have dinner together tomorrow night."

Kathy blinked, then glanced up. How long had she been standing in the middle of Dakota's living room? And how long had he been watching her? "To synchronize our plan?"

"To get used to each other." He placed several empty glasses on top of the bar. "We can't go to Asterland like this. Acting like strangers. No one will buy our cover."

She let out an anxious breath. Right. The reconciled couple. The Foreign Service consular and her husband. "We still have some details to work out about the mission."

"We can do that over dinner. Which means avoiding a

restaurant. There are too many ears out there. I don't want to take the chance of being overheard.''

And she didn't want to have dinner with him at the ranch. She couldn't bear the familiarity. ''How about my hotel suite? We can order in.''

''That's fine.''

He walked her to the door, and as she turned to say good-bye, their eyes met.

Yes, she thought, struggling to hold his gaze, they needed to get used to each other. Three years, too many missions and a secret miscarriage had created a lot of distance between them. Pretending to be a reconciled couple wasn't going to be easy.

The following evening Kathy stood before a full-length mirror in her hotel room. She wore a white suit, gold jewelry and low heels. Reaching into her blouse, she lifted a long chain. Her wedding ring glittered on the end of it, a brilliant-cut diamond surrounded by emeralds. It was foolish, she knew, to wear it in such a manner, but she didn't have the strength to part with it completely.

It reminded her of wishes and dreams, a house full of children and growing old with the man she loved—a life where terrorists and gunrunners didn't take her husband away from home. As she slipped the chain inside her blouse, the ring thumped against her heart, out of sight but not out of mind.

Kathy tilted her head. Her hair was loose about her shoulders, the way Dakota liked it best. Quickly she twisted it into a neat chignon, her fingers working the heavy strands with deft precision. This wasn't about what Dakota liked. This was a business meeting, a professional dinner engagement.

When the room-service waiter delivered the meal, Kathy stood nearby, watching him set the table. Dakota would be arriving at any moment. She signed the bill and forced a smile, telling herself to relax. She had been in the company of dignitaries and heads of state. One tall, ex-military man, a dark-eyed Comanche, had no right to twist her stomach into a pretzel.

Five minutes after the waiter departed, a knock sounded at the door. She answered it, keeping her head high and her posture straight but not stiff. "Hello, Dakota."

"Hi." He smiled, a brief affection that gentled his rawboned features.

She used to kiss the scar on his chin, she thought. And the one on his belly, too.

Kathy took a step back. What a thing to invade her mind—that masculine stomach, rippling with hard-earned muscle.

"Come in. I took the liberty of ordering our meal ahead of time."

"Great." He walked into the suite, his voice more casual than she had expected. But when he made a beeline for the phone and began dismantling it, she realized his tone was for show.

He talked about insignificant things as he swept the set of rooms for bugs, electronic devices that might have been planted by someone posing as part of the hotel staff. Kathy had already done a search, but she appreciated Dakota's professionalism. With her anxious behavior, she could have missed something. She wasn't accustomed to providing her own security.

"What are we having?" he asked, indicating his search had turned up clean.

"Prime rib," she responded, wishing she could relax the way a proper hostess should.

Tonight Dakota looked a little dangerous—black trousers, a black jacket and eyes as dark as his clothes. He used to complain that he didn't blend in well, that men in his field shouldn't stand out in a crowd. Of course, men in his field were masters of disguise, and he played the game to perfection. Kathy knew he had altered his appearance many times, his height the only feature he couldn't change.

"It smells good," he said.

"Yes, it does."

He scooted back her chair, and she took her seat, thinking they weren't off to a very good start. There was no level of comfort between them. None whatsoever.

She poured the wine, her hand steadier than her heart. He sat across from her, watching every move she made, his gaze filled with questions. Clearly he wanted to know why she had left.

Kathy wasn't ready to talk about personal matters, wasn't sure if it would even matter. Retired or not, Lieutenant Dakota Lewis was, and always would be, the ultimate soldier—a man drawn to the heat of battle. A wife longing for babies and domestic bliss had no place in his life.

Dakota reached for his wine, and Kathy toyed with her salad. But before the silence threatened to swallow them, he spoke. "Tell me about your relationship with the royal family."

"I consider Queen Nicole a friend," she answered, relaxing a little. "She is part American and enjoys having another American woman to talk to. Although she was born in Asterland, she was educated in the States and has a fondness for our culture."

"When were you assigned to the consulate in Asterland? You've been in Washington for the last three years."

So he knew where she had been. Well, of course he did. She couldn't very well hide from a man like Dakota, nor had she intended to. She had wanted him to come to her, wanted him to profess that she was more important than his work, that he would retire for good.

"I wasn't assigned to Asterland. I was brought in to handle a situation that involved Prince Eric." Queen Nicole's young son, a dark-haired little boy who had stolen Kathy's heart. "Prince Eric had gotten into trouble at a prestigious New England boarding school. He was on the verge of being suspended because his classroom behavior was too disruptive. And since the school officials weren't being particularly cooperative, Queen Nicole requested that an American consular assess the situation and report to her."

Dakota cut into his meat. "Your report must have impressed the queen."

"Prince Eric turned out to be a delightful child, which led me to believe his classroom behavior needed further investigation.'' Kathy adjusted the linen napkin on her lap. ''With the queen's approval, I brought in an educational psychologist. And the psychologist diagnosed Prince Eric with attention deficit disorder. Personally, I feel the boy had been treated unfairly. A learning disability isn't something that warrants a suspension.''

Dakota smiled. ''You've always been tuned in to kids. You could have been a teacher.''

Or a mother, she thought, swallowing the lump in her throat. Prince Eric had come into her life soon after the miscarriage, and bonding with the young boy had helped ease the pain of losing her own child. ''The queen transferred him to a boarding school that specializes in learning disabilities. He's doing well now. A determined fifth-grader.''

''It's hard to believe Prince Ivan came from the same family.''

''I know.'' Kathy pictured Prince Ivan. He was Eric's older brother, a grown man who abused his power and shamed his family. He had also been a menace to the town of Royal, a threat to the Cattleman's Club. But in the end, a cowardly act had consumed him. Rather than return to Asterland to face his family, the prince had committed suicide. ''Ivan is dead now.''

Dakota placed his fork on the table. ''But he's still creating trouble. Or his past deeds are. He's the one who convinced the king to appoint Payune to the position of Grand Minister. Payune and Ivan were thick as thieves.''

And at one time, the king, clearly blinded by parental love, had intended to abdicate the throne to Ivan. ''Prince Eric is nothing like his brother. He will make a fine king someday.''

''That's good to know. But if we don't stop Payune, young Eric will never get that chance.'' Dakota trapped her gaze, his dark eyes riveting. ''I hope to God Payune buys my cover. And yours, too. I'm going to have to convince him that you're a double agent.''

Kathy tried to look away, but couldn't. Dakota held her there, caught in his magnetic gaze. She wasn't able to respond; her mouth had gone dry. She reached for her wine, took a small sip.

His husky voice sounded gentle, low. "I'm sorry, sweetheart. I hate doing this to you, but I don't know how else to reach Payune."

Sweetheart. Kathy felt a pool of warmth settle deep in her belly. Dakota had used that endearment the first time they'd made love.

Show me what you like, sweetheart. Put my hands—

Oh yes, those hands. Those strong, callused hands—fingertips stroking her breasts, sliding lower, slipping between her thighs. He used to watch her climax, smile and watch, masculine pleasure alight in his dark eyes. Afterward they would kiss, and he would enter her, push himself deep inside, make it happen all over again. Every explosive, glorious sensation.

"Kathy?"

She started. "Yes?"

"Are you all right? Did that upset you?"

Yes, she wanted to say. It unnerves me that I can't stop thinking about us. That I can recall your touch, your smile, the feel of your mouth covering mine, the weight of your body, the rock of your hips. "No. I came into this mission knowing we would have to fool Payune. I'm prepared to play my part."

"You're absolutely sure? You don't have any second thoughts?"

"I'm ready for this assignment," she said, struggling to maintain her composure. "Aaron briefed me on all of the details." Dakota would present himself as a Texas billionaire willing to fund Payune's revolution for personal gain. And she would be painted as Dakota's shrewd wife—a woman who used a government job to her best advantage.

"Don't worry about me," she added. She wouldn't allow her thoughts to stray, wouldn't allow those disturbing images to cloud her mind. Because recalling Dakota's touch was possibly more dangerous than the mission.

Two

Kathy wore her hair up again, Dakota noticed, but the dry Texas wind had disturbed it, loosening several long, bright strands. She wore casual clothes—jeans and a short-sleeved cotton blouse, her shoulder nearly brushing his.

A bronze statue of Tex Langley, the founder of the Texas Cattleman's Club, stood like a monument behind them.

They sat on a park bench, but they weren't lounging on a leisure day. This was business, another meeting place where they wouldn't be overheard.

Sheikh Ben Rassad and his wife, Jamie, sat on the other side of the bench, a newly married couple looking far too much in love. Dakota resisted the urge to move closer to Kathy, to allow their bodies to touch. Although last night's dinner hadn't been a failure, it wasn't a complete success, either. They weren't exactly used to each other yet.

Dakota dug a booted heel into the grass. Maybe he should just kiss her and get it over with. Pull her onto his lap. Tug her hair loose. Slam his tongue into her mouth and devour the woman he had married.

After all, she was still technically his wife.

He glanced up at Ben Rassad. Yeah, right. Kiss Kathy now, here at the park, in front of his happily married friend. What the hell was he trying to prove? That he was an egotistical, envious idiot?

Dakota lifted a bottle of water and brought it to his lips, wetting his mouth and cooling his thoughts. Strange how things had worked out for Ben. The sheikh had been assigned to watch over Jamie when she needed protection, then ended up falling for her in the process. The feisty young woman had originally been a mail-order bride for Albert Payune, a union arranged by Jamie's father and Payune himself.

Luckily, Payune had backed out of the deal and never pursued Jamie any further. Which, in turn, had prompted this meeting—second-guessing Payune's actions—the man Dakota intended to take down.

"So, do either one of you have any idea why Payune had advertised for an American wife?" he asked, dividing his gaze between the other couple.

Jamie shook her head. "No, but we've talked about it. Tossed ideas back and forth."

"Like what, for instance?"

"Vanity, perhaps," Ben said. "Payune may have desired a young wife to boost his ego. Texas women are renowned for their beauty." He reached for Jamie's hand and held it lightly. "But there is also the possibility of revenge. Payune might blame the town of Royal for Ivan's suicide, and he planned to take one of our women as payment."

Dakota mulled over Ben's words, deciding anything was possible where Payune was concerned.

"I tend to think Sheikh Rassad was right the first time," Kathy said. "That Payune's ego was involved."

"Really?" When Dakota turned toward her, his hand brushed hers—an accidental touch that sent an electrical charge straight to his heart. He forced himself to concentrate on the discussion, but failed miserably. He noticed Kathy's hand was bare. She wore no rings. The wedding band he'd placed on her finger was gone.

Dakota looked over at Ben and Jamie. Both sat patiently as though waiting for Kathy to expound on her theory. Apparently he was the only one losing his train of thought. Damn it. He knew better than to allow his heart to get tangled up in this mission. Kathy had left him, and that was that.

Tightening his jaw, he turned toward her again. "So you think Payune wanted an American wife to make himself look good?"

She nodded. "It would enhance his public image in Asterland. Queen Nicole is well received in her country. And since she is part American, Payune may have been trying to find a wife he considered comparable to her." She shifted her gaze to Ben. "A beautiful Texan, just as Sheikh Rassad pointed out."

Dakota frowned. "If that's the case, then why did Payune let Jamie go? My contact in Asterland says he's no longer pursuing a wife, American or otherwise."

Kathy smoothed the wind-blown strands of her hair. "I don't know. But I've always had the feeling that Payune is enamored of Queen Nicole. Of course she's madly in love with her husband. She isn't the kind of woman to have an affair, and I'm sure Payune knows that."

"But he wants her." And in Dakota's opinion that made Albert Payune even more dangerous. Could there be an assassination plot brewing? If the king were killed during the revolution, Queen Nicole would be left a widow, free to accept Payune's affection. And if Payune controlled the queen and Prince Eric, then, in a sense, he would control Asterland, too.

Dakota figured Payune had three options: overthrow the Asterland government through a revolution, dispose of the entire royal family or kill the king and marry Queen Nicole.

But how could Payune possibly think the queen would turn to him? If she loved her husband, she wouldn't embrace the man who had assassinated him.

Or would she? Was Kathy wrong about Queen Nicole? Maybe the queen wasn't as madly in love as she claimed to be.

Wives, it seemed, changed their minds about such matters. Dakota knew firsthand that love wasn't all it was cracked up to be.

They were both experienced flyers—more than experienced. Kathy had lived abroad most of her life, and Dakota was a pilot, a man who belonged to the sky. But not today. Although they rode on a private, luxurious jet owned by a prominent member of the Cattleman's Club, they were anything but relaxed.

The pilot, thank God, was another retired air force officer, someone Dakota trusted implicitly. Flying to Asterland with Kathy was difficult enough, and the last thing Dakota needed to concern himself with was the competency of their pilot.

Kathy sat across from him in a cushioned chair. The jet offered an upscale, home-like setting, a penthouse apartment in the sky. Kathy fit right in. Dakota supposed he did, too—on the outside at least. He'd been born into money, even if he was the bastard son of a hard-nosed land baron, a man who'd left him a sizable inheritance. Dakota didn't fashion himself after his father, but he'd done his damnedest to earn the older man's respect.

Kathy paged through a magazine. It wasn't difficult to assess that she wasn't absorbed in its contents. Her mind was elsewhere. And rightly so, Dakota supposed. This mission had sucked both of them in, drawing them into an imminent vacuum.

Placing the magazine on a table, she looked up and asked, "Are you sure we're doing the right thing?"

Good God. She had second thoughts? Now? They were halfway to Asterland. "What do you mean?"

"Not involving the king and queen. I don't like deceiving them."

"We're not deceiving them. We're keeping this mission under wraps to protect them. The less people involved, the safer we'll all be."

Kathy frowned. "But it's their country."

And she was thinking with her heart instead of her head,

Dakota thought. Her friendship with the queen was blinding her judgment. "Kathy, we don't know how many cabinet members are actually part of the revolution plot. If the king or queen put their trust in the wrong person, it would blow our operation sky-high. We can't take that chance."

And Dakota had some concerns about Queen Nicole and Albert Payune. "Besides, how well do you really know the queen? She could have stumbled into an affair with Payune. That might be the reason he quit looking for a wife."

Kathy narrowed her eyes. "Queen Nicole hasn't *stumbled* into affair, Dakota. I already told you she wouldn't do something like that. She loves her husband."

And I thought you loved me, he wanted to say. "So women don't cheat on their husbands? They don't get themselves tangled up with other men?"

"Some do, I suppose. But not most. That's a man's game."

She picked up the magazine again, and Dakota kicked his legs out in front of him. A man's game. Right. He hadn't even looked at another women since she'd been gone. He studied Kathy's professional attire, her slim, fashionable figure. When she flipped a page, he caught sight of a gold band glinting on her finger. She wore her wedding ring, the diamond and emerald design he'd had custom made for her.

Don't take that as encouragement, he told himself. She'd put it back on for show, for the sake of their cover. "So have you been with anyone?" he asked, his voice gruff. "Did you leave me so you could sleep with another man?"

Kathy's complexion paled. "I can't believe you're asking me something like that."

He felt his muscles tense. Technically, they were still married. Neither had filed for a legal separation, much less a divorce. He had a right to know. "Well?"

"Of course not." She lifted her chin and met his gaze, her eyes locking onto his. "What about you? Have you been with someone?"

"No." He shook his head and made light of his loneliness, the years he'd waited for her to return. "The way I figure it,

we've still got that piece of paper between us." As well as
the vows they had taken.

For better or worse. Until death do us part. He had meant
every word.

She let out an audible breath, her eloquent vocal skills suddenly failing her. "I suppose it was best that we...discussed
this issue. I...we...don't need any personal distractions on
this mission."

Yeah, and wondering if your spouse had a new lover would
certainly fall under the category of a personal distraction. "I
agree. Now that it's out in the open, I won't mention it
again."

"Good."

Her smile was tight, but the fear in her eyes had faded.
Fear that he had been with another woman. The thought made
him a little smug, as well as confused. If things like that still
mattered, why hadn't she come home before now?

Dakota dragged a hand through his hair. She isn't home,
Lieutenant Lewis. This is an assignment, a fake reconciliation.
Get your facts straight.

They remained silent for the next twenty minutes, she, oc-
cupying herself with another magazine, he, staring out the
window at the night sky. He would have rather been piloting
the plane than sitting idle, thinking about how much he
missed a closeness with his wife. Sure, they had spent some
time away from each other, but due to the nature of his work,
those separations couldn't be helped. And their reunions used
to be nice. Damn nice. Nothing like this one.

"Dakota?"

He turned away from the window. "Yes?"

"Why didn't you ever tell me the Lone Star jewels really
existed?"

While he'd been thinking about her, she'd been thinking
about the recovered jewels. Well, at least one of them had
her mind on the mission. "Only those associated with the
Texas Cattleman's Club were supposed to know they existed."

"Because of the legend?"

"Yes."

"So the story about that soldier is true?"

Dakota nodded. A Texas soldier had found the jewels during the War with Mexico and had brought them to Royal after the war, intending to sell them and make his fortune.

"When he came home, oil was found on his land. So he believed just owning the stones was lucky, and that they should remain in Royal."

"And now the Cattleman's Club protects them, and everyone else thinks their existence is just a legend. A story passed down from generation to generation."

"Yes, but Payune came across the truth somehow."

Kathy leaned forward, clearly engrossed in their conversation. But then she loved jewels, and the Lone Star gems were a rare, stunning collection. Too bad she would never see them, he thought. He would enjoy watching her eyes glow—those gorgeous green eyes.

"Any idea how Payune found out about them?" she asked.

"It's possible Prince Ivan had something to do with it. When he was in Royal, he asked a lot of questions. It would stand to reason that he heard about the legend. He probably told Payune about it."

"And Payune discovered the legend was true, from his comrade, Robert Klimt—the man who had stolen the jewels." Kathy reclined in her chair. "I'm so glad they were recovered. They haven't been safeguarded all these years to end up in the wrong hands."

"Funding a revolution no less." Dakota rose and headed toward a small wet bar. "Do you want a cold drink?" he asked.

She shook her head.

"Then how about a cup of hot tea?" He knew she added one teaspoon of sugar and a splash of cream to her tea. He wondered if she remembered little details about him or if she had chosen to forget. It wouldn't be hard to recall that he drank his coffee black or that he considered hot sauce a breakfast staple.

"No, thank you. I'm fine."

He poured himself a tall glass of soda water and returned to his seat.

Kathy placed the magazine on her lap. "Are you concerned about the queen's ball? I know how much you dislike social functions."

Dakota cocked an eyebrow at her. He didn't dislike all social functions, just the ones that required a tuxedo and served champagne instead of beer.

"No, I'm not concerned about it. I've been to plenty of fancy affairs." And they made him uncomfortable as hell, even the familiar Texas Cattleman's Club events. Dakota had spent more years in war paint and combat gear than he had in uniform. This ball, he figured, would be the worst part of the mission. Next to Kathy, he would probably look like a big, snorting Brahma. James Bond he wasn't. Not all under-cover agents were that damned debonair.

"So you don't want me to brief you on royal protocol?" she asked.

Dakota scowled. "No, Miss friend-of-the-queen, I don't. I know how to behave around royalty. As you might recall, I spent twenty years of my life serving in the United States Air Force. I've picked up a few manners along the way."

She nibbled her bottom lip, then broke into an amused smile. "Miss friend-of-the-queen?"

He couldn't help but return her smile. Kathy knew him better than anyone. She knew darn well how he felt about attending the queen's birthday ball. "If the glass slipper fits, Lady Katherine."

She tossed her magazine at him. He ducked and shot her a playful grin, recalling how many times he used to tickle her on the living-room floor.

Dakota picked up the magazine, his grin fading. Somehow those tickling sessions would inevitably turn into foreplay. Hot, sexy kisses. Rubbing against each other through their clothes.

He looked over at Kathy and noticed her smile had dis-appeared, too. Just as well, he thought. The less tender memories they made, the better. Because when this assignment ended, they wouldn't be going home together.

The cottage the queen provided sat on a grassy cliff, the ocean below crashing upon a private stretch of beach. A cool, yet comfortable, sea breeze misted the May air, and clouds drifted lazily across an azure sky.

Kathy had stayed in the isolated cottage on several other occasions, and she adored the quaint, European charm. Window boxes displayed an arrangement of colorful flowers, and leafy vines clung to a white trellis. A scattered-stone walkway led to the front door. Inside was a collection of art and antiques, a cozy living area, two bedrooms, a fully stocked kitchen and two bathrooms decorated with hand-painted fixtures. French doors in each bedroom opened onto a lush, well-tended garden. A wrought-iron table sat amid perennial blooms in what Kathy considered an outdoor breakfast nook—a place to sip coffee and breathe the sea air.

The first thing Dakota did was search the cottage for concealed microphones, but Kathy expected as much. A frown furrowed his brow, she noticed. Was he preoccupied with the mission, or had he noticed the romantic ambiance—the vases of long-stemmed roses, the extravagant chocolates placed upon the master-bedroom bed? The big, quilted bed the queen's servants must have assumed Kathy and Dakota would be sharing?

He completed the search, and she stood beside their luggage. "We won't have daily maid service," she said. "There's a little bungalow behind the garden that was built as servant's quarters, but it's vacant. We've been provided with enough food, towels and linens to last through the week."

"Good. The less people around the better." He turned to look at her. "How did you manage that, anyway?"

"I informed the queen we wanted to be alone. She's fanatical about seeing to her guests' personal needs."

He frowned again. "Of course, our cover. Sorry, it was a stupid question."

With an answer that made them both wary, she realized. A married couple requesting privacy meant long, sensual baths, sipping wine by candlelight, feeding each other aphrodisiacs.

"I'll take the smaller bedroom," he said.

Kathy didn't respond, instead she followed him as he lifted her luggage and carried it to the master bedroom.

He placed her suitcase and garment bag on the bed, then turned toward the French doors and gazed out. "It's pretty here."

She moved to stand beside him. "There's a fountain in the center of the garden." And she thought of it as her own private wishing well, even if her wishes had yet to come true. "This cottage is in a world of its own."

"But it's not our world." With rigid shoulders, he turned away from the view, his mood switching from light to dark in one abrupt motion. "I have to meet with my contact soon. We can't get caught up in flowers and fountains. We're not on a holiday."

"I'm well aware of why we're here." Angry now, she continued to study the foliage. She wouldn't allow him to spoil the allure of her garden, a place where mystical creatures made magic. She wanted to believe that fairies fluttered around the flowers, and mermaids splashed in the ocean below.

"Kathy?"

She turned toward him with a hard stare. "What?"

He handed her one of the chocolates from the bed, an apology in his voice. "Truffles. They're your favorite."

She bit into the candy and savored the richness, the gentleness in his tone. "Is that why you offered me this room?" A silk-draped room with all the elements Kathy adored—scented candles, fresh-cut flowers, lace-trimmed sheers.

He smiled, but it fell short of reaching his eyes. He was worried, she realized. Worried about the mission, worried about being in an isolated cottage with his estranged wife. There was still so much distance between them, so much unnamed hurt. But how could she tell him that he hadn't loved her enough? That she needed more?

"You should unpack and get settled in," he said.

"I will." She searched his gaze. "Who is your contact, Dakota? Have I met him before?"

He shook his head. "No, but he's someone I've known a long time. A former intelligence officer, another skin."

Kathy knew that meant Dakota's contact was Native American. "Comanche?" she asked.

"Apache. Goes by the name Thunder. If something goes wrong on this assignment, he'll get in touch with you, Kathy. He vowed to look after you."

She didn't want to think about something going wrong, but she couldn't pretend the danger wasn't real. A man in Royal had been murdered by one of Payune's anarchists, and now they were on Payune's soil.

"Is Thunder a mercenary?" She knew Dakota didn't consider himself a mercenary because serving merely for pay wasn't his objective.

Dakota nodded. "Yes, but that doesn't make him someone you can't trust. He took a bullet for me. I owe him my life. We even look similar, like brothers."

Feeling an emotional chill, she crossed her arms. How many bullets had Dakota dodged? How many times had his life been spared? "Do you want me to unpack for you?" she asked, hoping he would understand why she had offered. She needed to place his clothes in the closet, his shaving gear in the bathroom. She used to unpack for him whenever he came home from an assignment. To her it meant he would be staying, at least for a while.

He didn't answer. Instead he remained motionless, staring at her. Her husband stood so close, she could see every eyelash, every pore in his sun-baked skin. And now she remembered how it felt to stroke his face. That intense face—smooth in some areas, rough in others.

Kathy moistened her lips. She wanted to grip his shoulders, lean into him and press her body against all that male hardness, feel her bones dissolve while his tongue stroked hers.

"You better go," she heard herself say.

She had no right to want him, not now, not after all the

tears she had cried, the baby she had lost. Dakota would forever be walking away. There would always be another assignment, another mission—something more important than his marriage.

He left the cottage, and she decided not to unpack for him. Touching his clothes would only make her ache.

Hours later Dakota returned from his meeting to find Kathy in the garden. Rather than disturb the moment, he watched her. She stood beside the fountain, wearing a pale cotton dress that billowed softly in the breeze. Her hair fell loose from its confinement, long silky strands framing her profile. She belonged in the setting, he thought. The foliage reached out to her, colorful blooms and lush greenery graced by her presence.

He felt like an intruder. But he had some news, and it couldn't wait. Bad news, it seemed, never could.

"Kathy?" he said softly.

She turned. "Oh, hi. I didn't know you were back."

"I haven't been here long." He hated to spoil the serenity, the beauty of what he had come to think of as her garden. Her enchanted garden. He had no right to be there. Dakota wasn't a dreamer. To him life consisted of reality—hard, strong doses of it.

"Any new information?" she asked.

He nodded. "A valuable necklace was stolen last night, and Thunder is convinced Payune is responsible." Dakota shifted his stance. "It belonged to the Duchess of Olin. A rare ruby heirloom that will command a substantial price on the black market."

"Now Payune has another means to fund his revolution."

"That's right. He couldn't get his hands on the Lone Star jewels, so he went after the next best thing."

Kathy frowned. "How are we going to get around this? You can't very well infiltrate Payune's operation if he doesn't need the money you intend to offer."

"True. But Payune is still powerless until he fences the necklace." Dakota felt a surge of adrenaline rush through his veins, nervous energy he couldn't shake. This mission had become even riskier, and his wife was his partner. That thought didn't sit well. "I have to retrieve the necklace. Steal it back, so to speak."

Kathy's face paled. "How's that going to work? Payune will become suspicious of everyone who comes into contact with him. If the necklace is taken from him, he'll know that someone is trying to stop him from funding the revolution. And it won't take him long to look in your direction, not once you approach him with your cover."

"This won't affect my cover." Dakota resisted the urge to pace, to stalk the garden path. "The Duchess has a paste copy of the necklace. It's the one she wears in public, and it's extremely high quality—identical to the original. So all I have to do is switch them. Payune will never know he was robbed."

"Not until he tries to fence it and discovers it's fake."

"True, but that's the beauty of this plan." Because Kathy was still frowning, Dakota sent her a roguish grin. "Payune will think he nabbed the wrong necklace to begin with, rather than suspect foul play."

She chewed her bottom lip. "It could work."

"It has to. We don't have much time. Thunder thinks the necklace will be fenced right after the ball. Late that night. He has a pretty good handle on who's backing the sale."

"The ball is three days from now."

"Which is why I've secured a meeting with Payune tomorrow. I need to establish my cover before he tries to sell the necklace. If I wait to approach him, he just might put two and two together."

A light breeze blew the loose stands of Kathy's hair. "When are you going to switch the necklaces? You have to do it before the ball."

"Don't worry about it, sweetheart. I'll let you know when I've got the details worked out." Dakota was going to need her help. And Thunder's, too. It would take the three of them to pull this off.

He motioned toward the stone path leading back to the

cottage. "Why don't we go inside? I could use a cup of coffee." He had more news. Something that would take an emotional toll on Kathy, something he hated to tell her.

While Kathy brewed a pot of coffee, a wave of homesickness washed over Dakota. Not for Texas, but for her. He missed having her nearby, watching her do simple tasks. Her feet were bare, and more of her hair had come loose. He could almost imagine them snuggling in front of the TV, eating popcorn the way they used to.

Life had never been particularly simple for Dakota, but being married to Kathy made the world a better place. She brought out the good in him. Or at least he'd thought so. Kathy must have felt differently. A woman didn't leave a good man.

She handed him a cup of the dark brew. He carried it into the living room while she doctored hers with sugar and cream.

He lowered himself onto the sofa, and she entered the room and sat across from him in an overstuffed chair.

"I can tell there's something else going on," she said. "What is it?"

"You won't like it."

"Dakota. Quit stalling. That isn't like you."

"You're right." He wondered why he was trying to protect her from someone else's life. "There are rumors circulating about the king and queen."

She placed her coffee on a nearby table. "What kind of rumors?"

"That their marriage is in trouble."

She pushed a stray lock of hair away from her face, her posture suddenly tense. "I don't believe it. People like to make things up. Create scandals. That happens to every royal family."

"Don't hide your head in the sand, Kathy. Plenty of couples have problems. And royalty are like everyone else in that regard." Our marriage failed, he wanted to say. And we were supposed to be happy. Why not a king and queen?

She thrust her chin in a stubborn gesture. "This does not mean Queen Nicole is having an affair with Payune."

"I didn't say it did."

"But that's what you're thinking."

"No, it's not." He was thinking about his own life, about why Kathy had walked out on him. He wished to hell he knew what he had done wrong. But now wasn't the time to ask. Dakota had to concentrate on retrieving the stolen necklace, on trapping the revolutionists and sending them to jail.

This mission wasn't about the hole in his heart. It wasn't about the woman seated across from him, messy locks spilling out of her proper hairdo, her long slim body draped in a summer cotton dress. This romantic little cottage wasn't home, and he would do well to remind himself of that. Every chance he got.

Three

Kathy couldn't sleep. Tired of tossing and turning, she slipped out of bed, then stood before the French doors. She knew her garden was out there, and beyond it a grassy terrain dotted with wildflowers. Below the hills, a midnight ocean crashed upon the shore. She gazed out, but it was too dark to see anything but an eerie reflection of herself.

A woman in white silk, her hair a long, tousled curtain. She looked like a mysterious shadow. A faded image. The silhouette of a lady longing for her lover.

Suddenly she could see this woman, this shadow of herself, roaming the hills, the wind whipping through the night, a sheer nightgown clinging to her skin. She was naked beneath the gown, waiting for her lover to come to her. He was forbidden, she knew. But she wanted him. Wanted to tumble to the ground with him, tear at his clothes and feel his mouth ravage hers.

What am I doing?

Shaking off a sexual chill, Kathy reached for her robe. A thirty-two-year-old woman should know better.

What she needed was food. A sandwich might be a poor substitute for a good night's rest, but it would keep her mind off foolish fantasies.

Belting her robe, she made her way to the kitchen. She flipped on the light. The room was spotless. The appliances were white, the wallpaper a tiny floral pattern. The appeal was homey, but kitchens usually were.

Kathy opened the refrigerator and removed a package of ham. After spreading a small amount of mayonnaise on two slices of bread, she reached for the mustard. It was her favorite—a spicy French condiment. In her haste to combine the two flavors, she ended up with a glob on her finger. Lifting it to her mouth, she froze. The chill returned. This time it slid down her spine like a masculine hand brushing her skin.

She was being watched. She could feel his eyes on her. She hadn't heard him come into the room, but she felt him there.

Watching every move she made.

She squared her shoulders and turned. He stood in the open doorway, tall and silent, his stare dark and intense. He wore a pair of drawstring sweat pants, riding low enough to expose his navel. He looked big and powerful, almost frightening. His eyes were so black, his pupils no longer existed. He had spiked his hair with restless hands, the glossy strands a startling shade of midnight blue. A trick from the light, but it startled her just the same.

The muscles along his stomach rippled with each breath he took. Hard, barely controlled breaths.

He was angry. Or aroused. Neither thought gave her much comfort.

She wanted to leave the kitchen, retreat to the safety of her room. But she couldn't. Her sandwich was half made, and Dakota blocked the doorway. She had no choice but to continue her task, to convince herself his presence hadn't unnerved her.

"I can't sleep," he said.

Turning back to her sandwich, she barely glanced up.

"Neither can I. But then we both drank coffee later than we should have."

Although she avoided his gaze, she knew it remained fixed on her. He couldn't know about her fantasy, about what her imagination had conjured, yet she sensed he did. In her mind, she had been waiting for her lover. Her forbidden lover. And now he was here—the man she wasn't supposed to want.

The coffee hadn't kept him awake, Dakota thought. She had.

It had been three years. Three years since he'd made love, since he'd felt her warm, willing heat. And she stood in the kitchen wearing a silky robe, her hair spilling gloriously over her shoulders—that fire-tinted hair he ached to grasp, lift to his face.

She didn't look his way. Instead she continued to make her sandwich. No, he couldn't sleep. Because he had tossed and turned, remembering every kiss, every tantalizing taste. He had even considered going outside, walking the cliffs as if he would find her there. As if she would be waiting.

"Maybe I should eat, too," he said. He wasn't hungry, but he couldn't think of another excuse to get close to her, to stand beside her and torture the hell out of himself.

"Oh, okay." She moved to allow him room at the butcher-block isle.

He came forward, grazing her shoulder as he reached for the bread. She slipped by him to rinse a tomato. And when she turned back, her robe fell open.

He wasn't a painter, a man who made images come to life, but at this moment, this incredible, breathtaking moment, he sought to immortalize her. Kathy's nightgown was as filmy as a lace curtain, as sheer as a summer rain. Her nipples brushed the surface, and he imagined the fabric cool and sleek against her skin.

He lifted his head, and their gazes collided. The tomato fell from her hand and rolled onto the butcher block. And then nothing moved. Nothing made a sound.

"What's happening?" she whispered, her voice barely audible.

He heard her, yet he didn't. Her robe was still open, and heat rose between their bodies like steam. He knew they fought to breathe the same air.

Outside the wind grew angry with lust, forcing its way through the trees. He could hear it rattling the windows.

He fought the urge to push her to the floor, tumble and roll, tear at the wisp of silk and lace she wore. Wild, forbidden lovemaking. The wind was challenging him to take her. His loins hardened, his pulse quickened, his mouth went dry. He moistened his lips and imagined tasting hers.

What's happening?

The wind howled again, and Dakota gripped the counter. Damn the wind. Damn the ache in his groin. He stared at Kathy; she stared back at him. Her eyes shone like emeralds. Sensual. Catlike.

Damn her.

Damn them both.

"Nothing's happening," he said, masking the arousal in his voice, the huskiness that nearly made him hoarse. "Your robe came undone, and..."

She moved like lightning, a blur before his eyes. When he focused again, her robe was belted, snug and secure. She picked up the tomato as though trying to backtrack, make that other moment disappear.

She glanced at him quickly, then looked away. She couldn't meet his gaze, yet only moments ago those green eyes bore brazenly into his.

This was so damn awkward, he thought. It shouldn't be, but it was. He had seen every inch of her, caressed her most intimate places. They had showered together, licked beads of water off each other's skin. They weren't sexual strangers. Yet they were. Three years spanned between them—an eternity.

"Maybe we should talk about it."

"There's nothing to talk about." She studied the tomato she had cut into even little slices. "We're making sandwiches."

"I'm not hungry. I only said I wanted a sandwich so I

could get close to you. But I'm okay now. I got through it, and so did you.'' He tossed his bread in the trash. ''This is only our first night. We'll feel better in the morning. Normal.'' The wind would calm and the sexual pull would pass. Daylight would make everything all right.

She glanced up. ''Do you think so?''

He could hope. ''Sure. We just have to get used to each other.''

Much to his relief, Kathy smiled—a small, delicate tilt of her lips. ''Maybe I'll pass on the sandwich, too,'' she said. ''It's been a long day, and I could use some sleep.''

Dakota finally slept, not a deep, soundless sleep, but enough to help him function the following morning. He knew he would find Kathy in the kitchen. He could smell breakfast, the homey aroma of bacon sizzling and eggs frying.

He stood at the bathroom sink and splashed water on his face. A shower could wait. He couldn't recall the last time Kathy had cooked for him. It was a good sign, he thought. Apparently she had decided to put what had happened behind them.

As casually as possible, he entered the kitchen. ''Good morning. Is there anything I can do to help?''

She turned away from the stove, and for a moment, a suspended moment in time, their eyes met. And held.

He stood, riveted to the floor, the tiles cool against his feet. Don't let it happen again. Not now. Not today.

She blinked, and the air in his lungs whooshed out.

''You can set the table.''

''Sure. Okay.'' He opened the appropriate cabinet and removed the dishes. ''The bacon smells good. A great aroma to wake up to.''

''I figured we could both use a hearty breakfast.'' She motioned to the coffee pot. ''It's strong and dark, just the way you like it.''

''Thanks.'' Sidetracked now, he left the table half set. Pouring himself a mug of freshly perked coffee, he leaned against the counter and sipped. Was Kathy worried about his meeting with Payune? Was that the reason for this special treatment? Or was she trying to prove how normal staying in the same house could be?

Her hair was coiffed to perfection, he noticed, the fiery tresses twisted neatly, two pearl combs making an elegant statement. Her skin glowed flawlessly, her makeup applied with skill. She wasn't dressed to go out, but he sensed she would be before long.

Realizing breakfast was ready and he'd neglected his domestic duty, he gathered some silverware and napkins. The kitchen table matched the butcher-block isle, and a bay window presented a spectacular view.

She filled their plates and took a chair. He sat across from her and smiled. She had placed his favorite hot sauce on the table. Apparently she had supplied the queen's servants with a list of foods to provide, right down to brand name selections—items imported from a variety of continents.

He lifted the bottle, then poured the spicy sauce over his eggs. "You remembered."

"Of course," she responded in an easy voice. "How could I forget? You practically refuse to eat breakfast without it."

Was she as relaxed as she seemed? Or was she drawing from her social skills to fool him? Dakota thought Kathy would make a hell of a poker player. She could bluff with the best of them. He had no idea what was actually going on in her mind.

His one-track mind, on the other hand, had taken a dangerous turn. He imagined destroying her proper hairdo, bathing her lips with strawberry preserve, then licking it off with slow, erotic strokes. Apparently his social skills, as well as his table manners, weren't enviable qualities. It didn't take much to fuel his sexual appetite—a sunny kitchen and a tasty breakfast did him just fine. Now last night's haunting didn't seem quite so odd. The woman had been wearing see-through silk.

"Do you have an appointment later?" he asked.

"Tea with the queen. The palace is sending a car for me this afternoon."

A long, black limo, no doubt. He cocked his head. "That sounds downright snooty. Why didn't you tell me before now?"

She buttered her toast. "I always have tea with the queen when I'm invited to Asterland. This is nothing out of the ordinary. It won't arouse suspicion."

He shoveled a forkful of eggs into his mouth and swallowed, enjoying the trappings of a home-cooked meal. "Routine or not, you still have to keep me informed about everywhere you go, everything you do. Don't take anything for granted while we're here. Okay?"

She nodded solemnly. "Okay."

Dakota savored a slice of bacon, and Kathy added cream to her coffee, a drink he assumed she had diluted with extra water. He knew she preferred a milder brew.

She studied her cup, and he assumed her mind was on her audience with the queen.

Today they would both slip into their respective roles.

Hours later Dakota arrived at Albert Payune's home. A crenellated gateway, reminiscent of a medieval structure, led to the entrance of the Grand Minister's estate. The house itself wasn't quite so foreboding, but it reflected European craftsmanship with its stone-by-stone construction.

A butler escorted Dakota to a dimly lit office furnished with a large mahogany desk and leather wing-back chairs. But what caught Dakota's eye was an impressive collection of swords. Displayed on the paneled walls, they wielded military power, something Payune obviously admired.

"The Grand Minister will be with you shortly," the butler said, his English heavily accented.

"Thank you," Dakota responded, exaggerating his drawl. Today he was a big, tall, rich Texan—a businessman eager to make an unethical deal.

He didn't scan his surroundings for a safe. He knew Payune wouldn't keep the stolen necklace in his office. He would probably secure the heirloom jewels in his private quarters— the master suite where he slept. Thunder was working on a

diagram of the estate, so it wouldn't be long before Dakota
would have a floor plan to back up his instincts.

Minutes later Payune entered the room. A man in his early
fifties, he stood with his shoulders squared and his head held
high. He was neither tall nor broad. He was of medium height
with a medium build, his physique toned and trim. He wore
a dark suit with a silk ascot tie. And although his hair was
thinning, he wasn't foolish enough to style it in one of those
ridiculous comb-overs. Albert Payune carried his vanity with
pride. He had an impeccable quality about him, but power-
hungry rulers often did.

Payune extended his hand, and they exchanged a proper
greeting.

Dakota had dressed carefully for the occasion. He couldn't
present himself as a showy, loud-mouthed American, because
that would belie his military background. But he still wanted
to be easily identified with Payune's image of Texas, so he
had worn a pair of custom-made cowboy boots and a 5X
Royal Stetson he'd removed upon entering the house.

"Please, have a seat, Lieutenant Lewis."

"Thank you." Dakota settled into one of the wing-back
chairs while Payune walked around to the desk. Referring to
a retired officer by his rank was accepted as proper protocol,
and a man in Payune's position would naturally adhere to
decorum.

The butler appeared with a silver tray, offering both men
snifters of brandy. When the servant departed, Payune lifted
his eyes to Dakota.

"So you have come to discuss a business venture?"

"Yes, sir, I have." Dakota met the other man's detached
gaze. "My partners and I intend to open a resort in Asterland
with the biggest, grandest casino imaginable. But our only
stumbling block is King Bertram." And for the sake of this
mission, a proposal for the resort had been presented to the
Cabinet under the guise of a Texas corporation. A proposal
Dakota knew the king would not approve.

"I see." Payune swirled his brandy. "Am I to understand

that you want me to influence King Bertram to reconsider his stand on this matter?''

''In a manner of speaking.''

''You realize the king believes our country could not successfully support a venture such as yours. Our neighbors in Obersbourg have converted a portion of their palace into an exclusive gaming casino. How many resorts are tourists willing to visit? Asterland is still quite obscure.''

''So was Obersbourg before they opened their casino.'' And Dakota knew damn well Payune didn't intend to rule an obscure little country. He wanted to put himself and Asterland on the map. ''I'm talking about a full-scale resort—a five-star hotel, a spa, a country club and a PGA quality golf course. I have some of the wealthiest men in Texas in on this deal. And we don't intend to take no for an answer.''

Payune's demeanor was no longer detached. ''I've seen your proposal. And I must admit, it was quite impressive.''

''And so is the fact that you're going to govern Asterland someday.''

''You're mistaken. Prince Eric is heir to the throne.''

Dakota chose not to comment further. The Grand Minister was playing the loyal Cabinet member, feigning disinterest in the crown.

Payune placed his hands on the desk, then linked them together. ''As I said, the proposal for your resort was impressive, but I am puzzled by one thing.''

Dakota sipped his drink even though he had never acquired a taste for brandy. ''And what would that be?''

''Why, your wife, of course. Is she aware of your venture?''

Dakota's heart took a quick, forward leap. ''She's not only aware of it, she supports it without reserve.''

''But she is also a high-ranking Foreign Affairs consular.''

Dakota kept his gaze focused on his opponent. ''That's right, she is,'' he said, his tone implying Kathy used a government job to her best advantage. If Payune assumed Kathy's friendship with the royal family had been manipulated to influence the king to approve the resort, then all the better. But before the other man concentrated too deeply on Kathy, Dakota continued, "I was hoping, sir, that you would help me get this project off the ground. If anyone can make this happen, you can."

Payune sat with his head tilted at a regal angle. "I appreciate your confidence, but I do not see how I can."

"Maybe you could take some time to think it over." Dakota paused a beat, then leaned forward and dropped a hint about the impending revolution, making damn sure the other man wouldn't forget this meeting. "My partners and I are willing to make it worth your while." A cash settlement he hoped Payune would be in dire need of within a matter of days. "And with your involvement, I'm sure King Bertram would no longer stand in our way."

Kathy walked with Queen Nicole along a stone path. Both women adored flowers, and strolling the castle gardens after a tea had become one of their favorite moments to share. Azaleas, poppies, tulips, irises—Kathy couldn't begin to name them all. There were also bridges to cross, statues to admire, bodies of water rippling with sunlight.

"This is like stepping into a painting," Kathy said.

The queen smiled as they passed a lily pond, then stopped to breathe the country air. "And today we are in a Monet."

Kathy turned to look at her friend. She thought Queen Nicole was one of the most beautiful women she had ever seen. With jet black hair and violet-blue eyes, she could have been a model. Even at fifty-three, she had a face and figure cameras loved. But for Kathy there was no envy, only admiration.

"You have been quiet on this visit," the queen said. "Are you not well?"

"I'm fine. It's just been so long since I've shared a home with my husband." At least, she thought, that was a portion of the truth. She couldn't lead the queen to believe that her personal life was in perfect order, that her supposed reconciliation with Dakota had no flaws. The queen had come to know her too well for such a charade.

"You have not told him yet, have you?"

"About the miscarriage? No. And I'm not sure I can."

The other woman guided her toward a bench overlooking a sweep of irises. "If you want to have a life with him again, then you must."

But I'm only pretending I want a life with him, Kathy thought. So what good would it do to tell him about the baby? They couldn't alter the past. Dakota hadn't been there when she'd needed him. There was nothing either one of them could do that would change that.

"You could forgive him," the queen said as though reading her mind. "There is healing in forgiveness."

Kathy watched a butterfly light upon a flower. "I know." But how could she forgive him when she knew his work would always be more important than their marriage? "We're still attracted to each other." A dangerous attraction, she thought. "I can't think clearly when I'm around him."

No, she couldn't think, but she could feel. And fantasize.

She could still see herself waiting for him on the cliffs. Waiting for him to pull her to the ground, tear her nightgown and cover her body with his. And for one haunting moment last night, she knew he had wanted the same thing—desperate, forbidden lovemaking—a union they would have regretted later.

Queen Nicole sighed. "I have no right to give advice."

Jarred from her wayward thoughts, Kathy turned, then studied her friend's sad expression. "Forgive me for asking, but are the rumors true? Is your marriage troubled?"

"Yes, very troubled. Losing Ivan has put a strain on our relationship. The king refuses to mourn his son. He cannot cope with what Ivan did."

Kathy hadn't been prepared to discuss Prince Ivan, but she could see that the other woman needed to confide in someone—someone she trusted. "Most men don't grieve the way women do. They tend to keep their feelings inside."

Queen Nicole's voice quavered. "But the king is still too hurt and too angry to grieve. And until he forgives Ivan, our lives will never be the same." She lifted her face to the sun as though the warmth would help. "I, too, was destroyed by what Ivan had done. But he left us a note. He begged for our forgiveness.''

Kathy knew Prince Ivan had arranged a car accident that had taken the lives of a neighboring princess and her lover. Plus he'd tried to force the princess's sister, Anna, to marry him and merge their countries. So in remorse and shame, the Asterland prince had committed suicide rather than face his family. ''I'm sorry. I wish there was something I could say.''

''I grieved for my son when I buried him, and I found it in my heart to forgive him. I ask nothing more of the king.''

''I understand.''

Together they rose from the bench and walked side by side in companionable silence, the garden offering solace. Kathy had never doubted the queen's love for the king, nor had she suspected her of having an affair with Payune. And now Dakota could put aside his suspicion. What troubled the royal marriage was not another man.

Footsteps sounded on the walk, and a child with a radiant smile appeared. Ten-year-old Prince Eric had slipped through a path of trees, his fretful, red-faced nanny on his heels.

The queen laughed. ''He is so full of energy.''

And so beautiful, Kathy thought. The young prince had inherited his mother's jet-black hair and easy manner. His skin was tanned from the outdoor activities he enjoyed at his American boarding school, and his eyes were dark like the king's.

Like Dakota's.

Kathy realized Prince Eric looked the way she imagined a child of hers and Dakota's would look. Immediately she thought about the baby she had lost—the little boy or girl who should be toddling beside her.

''Mother, you told me I could visit with Kathy,'' the boy said.

''Yes, but I did not say you could give Nanny a wild goose chase.'' The queen cupped her son's cheeks, then whispered. ''Nanny is not so young anymore. You must show her the courtesy befitting her age.''

''Yes, ma'am,'' he responded.

Kathy knew the boy wanted to fidget. She couldn't help but smile. Prince Eric glanced over at her with a gleam in his dark eyes. When his mother released him, he came toward her with a proper greeting, and she responded in kind.

The hug that followed made her a little misty-eyed. "I've missed you, young sir."

"And I, you." He stood gazing up at her. "Mother says I may go to the ball. At least for a little while."

"I'm glad. I'll be there, too."

"Is your husband going to escort you?"

Kathy resisted the urge to skim his bangs from his eyes. "Yes, he is."

"So I will meet him?"

She thought of her lost child again. Dakota's child. "Yes," she said softly. "I would like very much for the two of you to meet."

Kathy sat beside Dakota in their rental vehicle, heading down a winding country road toward the beach. They had dressed for a casual outing, but Kathy assumed Dakota had business on his mind. They had a lot to discuss. The queen's birthday ball was tomorrow evening, and the necklace switch still hadn't been made.

Dakota parked the utility vehicle, and they remained silent for a moment. The private beach presented a narrow stretch of sand and a clear blue ocean bathing a scatter of large, jagged rocks.

Kathy smiled to herself. Mermaids lounged on the rocks when no one could see them, she thought—their long, luxurious hair blowing in the breeze, their iridescent tails swaying to the rhythm of the sea. Were there mermen? Or did the mermaids sing their siren's song for human males—men who didn't believe in fairy tales.

Men like Dakota.

"Let's go," he said.

He carried a blanket and a backpack, and she trudged beside him in a pair of lace-up boots. It wasn't a swimsuit day. The wind blew with a brisk chill, and the ocean roared with foaming waves. Both she and Dakota wore sweatshirts and jeans.

He picked a spot away from the tide and secured the blanket the best he could. They sat beside each other, and Kathy waited for him to speak. She could have kept silent for hours just watching the sea, imagining schools of glittery fish and sunken treasures sparkling with gold.

"Have you ever been through the maze at the palace?" he asked.

Kathy turned. "Just once. Prince Eric wanted me to play hide-and-seek with him, but I ended up getting lost. He had to rescue me, even though he was the one hiding. I felt a little foolish." And somewhat frightened. The garden maze was a labyrinth of tall, dark-green shrubs, a puzzle that had made her feel like Alice in Nightmareland.

"Did you ever make it to the center?"

She nodded. "Prince Eric guided me there." And she recalled a white gazebo, a porch-type swing and a lovely arrangement of seasonal blooms. "It was pretty, but not quite worth the trouble."

He frowned. "So you wouldn't remember how to get to the gazebo on your own?"

Kathy pushed a strand of hair away from her face. She had worn her hard-to-hold hair in a practical ponytail, but already wispy tendrils were coming loose. "Heavens, no." She studied the crease between his eyebrows. "Why? What's going on?"

"I'm going to switch the necklaces during the ball."

She had no idea what that had to do with the garden maze, but, regardless, his plan made no sense. "You can't. You're a guest at the ball. Nobody can be two places at once."

"It's the only time I can make the switch, the only time I can be absolutely certain of Payune's whereabouts." He sent her a wicked grin, his teeth gleaming. "And you're wrong, I can be in two places at once."

That slash of white in an otherwise dark face made him look like a rogue. She had to tell her girlish heart to behave. "I hope you're going to explain."

He moved closer. "Of course, I am. This plan involves you."

And that nightmarish maze, she thought with sudden doom. "Go ahead."

"Okay. We'll attend the ball—drink, dance and make our presence known to Payune. Then at 2030, we'll take a walk—stroll through the maze and neck a little on our way to the gazebo."

Her heart bumped. "Neck?"

The roguish grin returned. "Kiss, nibble, paw each other like lusty teenagers."

She couldn't catch her breath, so she forced herself to gulp the sea air. She didn't want to kiss him. Well, maybe she did. But because she did, she knew she shouldn't. "That's hardly proper behavior at a royal ball."

He raised an eyebrow at her. "Don't get your sequins in a snit, Kathy. This is part of the mission. Payune might be watching us. He may even decide to follow. But if he sees us wrapped in each other's arms, he'll figure we're just out on a romantic, moonlit stroll."

How did Dakota know her dress had sequins on it? she wondered testily, wishing she had brought an alternative ball gown. "Payune is going to be that suspicious of us? Enough to follow us outside?"

"Hell, yes. He's not a stupid man. He understood the direction I was taking yesterday. I'm a former air force officer from Royal, Texas, with a Foreign Service consular for a wife. And to top it off, we're asking to be part of his revolution." Dakota blew a windy breath. "I'd say that makes us the most interesting couple at the ball."

He was right, of course. But necking for the sake of the mission irked her. Everything Dakota did was for some top-secret assignment, and now that included kissing her. "So what happens next?"

"We go to the gazebo, retreat to a dark corner, and I slip away. From there I break into Payune's estate, switch the necklaces and return before anyone knows I'm gone."

Panic rose in her throat as the sound of the ocean crashed in her ears. "You're going to leave me in the maze? Alone?"

His voice gentled. "No, sweetheart. Thunder will take my place. In the dark, we're virtually twins. Same height, same body structure."

Wonderful. She would be trapped in the maze with a stranger while Dakota took all the risks. "Why can't Thunder switch the necklaces?"

"Because breaking and entering are my areas of expertise, not his."

Kathy got a mental picture of a cat burglar—a tall, shadowy figure dressed in black. Dakota would do his part, and she would have to do hers. "It's a good plan," she said, reminding herself the future of a country was at stake.

"Thanks." He removed a sheet of paper from his backpack, and it snapped in the wind. "Now all we have to do is memorize the key to the maze."

"Is that a diagram of it?" she asked, leaning toward the paper.

He nodded. "Looks like one of those magazine puzzles, doesn't it?"

"Yes, it does." The pattern of the hedges had been outlined, along with a red line marking a zigzag path to the gazebo. She assumed the resourceful mercenary named Thunder had provided it.

"Come sit here so we can study it together."

Here, Kathy realized, undoubtedly meant between those long, denim-clad legs and against that big, broad chest. She frowned at the map. Didn't he have another copy? "Why do we have to share?"

"So we can snuggle. Payune won't buy our cover if we flinch every time we touch." He adjusted his position to make room for her. "Since we have to get physical at the ball, we may as well get used to the idea now."

Sure. Right. For the sake of the mission, she thought, hiding her frown. Settling herself between his legs, she leaned back, then held her breath. In spite of the chill, a sudden, unwelcome heat blazed through her body.

"Relax," he whispered, slipping his arms around her waist.

She let out the breath she was holding and tried to focus on the sway of the ocean, the color of the sand, the sprinkle of broken sea shells surrounding their blanket. But her concentration wavered. All she could think about was the pressure of her bottom nestled between his thighs.

He moved closer and nuzzled her neck. He smelled like a familiar brand of aftershave, the one he had always worn. She swallowed and searched for a place to rest her hands.

"You still feel stiff," he said.

Well, so did he, she thought, lowering her hands to her own lap. But then his stiffness was beneath his zipper, and that probably didn't count.

"I'm fine," she responded. But when he tugged at her earlobe with his teeth, she wasn't fine. She wanted to turn her head and capture his mouth, remember the first time they had kissed. The last time. Every time in between.

He held the maze key out in front of her. The paper rippled in the wind. "Don't let it blow it away," he told her.

She grabbed it and held on for dear life. She felt him removing the decorative band from her hair, dislodging her ponytail. She knew he liked her hair loose, liked to run his hands through it, liked to mar her proper image.

"Do you still think about me, Kathy?"

In bed. He wanted to know if she climbed under the covers at night and thought about him, imagined the stroke of his tongue, the rock of his hips. That hard, powerful body thrusting into hers. "Yes."

He placed his hand over hers, then began tracing the pattern of the map. When his jaw brushed the side of her cheek, his beard stubble grazed her skin. "I think about you, too. About all the things I used to do to you." His voice turned low—hushed and aroused. "The naughty things you used to do to me."

Kathy moistened her lips.

The naughty things you used to do to me.

Suddenly the secluded beach called out to her—the allure of the wind, the scent of the sea, the passion of the sky. Now she remembered the last time they had made love. The way they had rolled over the bed, tugging at each other's clothes. His labored breathing, her hand closing over his arousal. The forceful kisses, the soft moans, the silky sensations. She had lowered her head to taste him, take him into her mouth while he'd fisted her unbound hair and raised his hips, his gaze following every urgent stroke.

"You used to watch," Kathy heard herself say. You watched that night, she thought, that wild, bittersweet night.

"And you used to make me crazy," he responded, scraping his jaw against her cheek once again. "So good. So crazy."

Her heartbeat thudded in time with his, but she knew he wouldn't kiss her, wouldn't ease the forbidden hunger flowing through their veins. Instead he would make them both wait until tomorrow night. The mission, Kathy thought. As much as they lusted after each other, they still needed an excuse—even for a kiss.

Four

────

Dakota walked down the hall, then stopped when he saw Kathy through her open doorway. She stood in front of a full-length mirror, checking her appearance. When she smoothed her dress, he allowed himself a long, languorous look.

The emerald-colored gown clung to her curves in a lithe, elegant shimmer. The fabric, a watery satin, caught the light each time she moved. The neckline, decorated with a row of sequins, revealed a hint of cleavage. Her skin looked warm and smooth next to all that icy green.

Her hair, he decided, had been styled with him in mind. It fell loose about her shoulders in thick, scarlet waves, both sides adorned with a diamond-and-emerald-studded comb. It appeared deliberately messy, yet fashionable. He could touch it, twine it around his fingers, lift it to his face, and no one would know. It was, Dakota thought with a smile, a hairstyle created for lovers.

When she turned his way, her hand flew to her heart. "Oh my God! You scared the daylights out of me. How long have you been standing there?"

Long enough to get turned on, he almost said, his smile tilting a little crookedly. "Just a few minutes."

Her eyes, he noticed, had been enhanced with a smoky liner. The dark, sultry illusion made them appear even more catlike. "You look incredible, Kathy."

She tilted her head, and diamonds winked at her ears. "Thank you."

She slipped into satin pumps, and he wondered what she had going on under her dress. A corset-type bra? Silk panties? A garter belt and thigh-high hose? He moved into the room so he could enjoy her mouthwatering scent. He knew she had layered her favorite body products: powder, lotion, a strawberry mist. She smelled good enough to eat, so he imagined lathering her with whipped cream—a taste from her nipples— a line down her belly—a sweet, sexy flavor between those long, gorgeous legs.

She would purr, he decided. Press herself against his mouth and make throaty little sounds.

When she glanced up, he shoved his hands in his pockets and feigned a casual air. He wasn't behaving like an officer or a gentleman. But damn it, he wanted her. Wanted to bathe her with the afterglow of a warm, wet orgasm.

"You look handsome, Dakota."

He blinked, his blood still pumping lust through his veins. Struggling to focus, he glanced at his starched white shirt. He wore a traditional black tux with a pair of onyx cufflinks. Kathy had always liked the way he looked in formal attire. "Oh, yes. Thanks."

She opened a sequin evening bag and placed a lace handkerchief, a gold compact and a tube of lipstick inside. Then reaching into the closet, she removed a shimmering green jacket that matched her sleeveless dress. "I'm ready."

They walked toward the front door, then he turned and headed into the kitchen. "I forgot something." Opening the fridge, he removed a windowed box. "It's a wrist corsage." A delicate floral design he couldn't resist—a white orchid with gold ribbon and a spray of baby's breath shimmering with emerald glitter.

"How did you know?" she asked, reaching for the flower, her voice soft with feminine wonder.

"That it would match your gown?" he watched her slip the corsage around her wrist. "I didn't. I ordered it because it reminded me of you." And because he knew it would complement the diamonds and emeralds sparkling on her finger—the engagement ring and wedding band he had given her.

An hour later they arrived at the palace, then stood with the other guests in a receiving line, waiting to pay their respects to the royal family. The king stood tall in a uniform that displayed his commander-in-chief status. Dakota assumed Payune drooled inwardly over that uniform, since the impressive armed forces rank came with the crown.

The queen glittered in a diamond tiara and a sparkling gown, and young Prince Eric wore a serious expression, even though boyish excitement brightened his dark eyes.

The ballroom dominated nearly an entire floor. Crystal chandeliers glimmered from the ceiling and leaded-glass doors led to the gardens. Tables in the dining area were set with candles, polished silver and fine linens. A velvet curtain with gold tie-backs signaled the entrance to the dance hall.

Dakota wasn't the least bit nervous, but he was no longer out of his element. Tonight's agenda put him in control. The ball was now a crucial part of the mission.

As the festivities got underway, Kathy spoke to a great number of people—most of them as noble as their prestigious European titles. Dakota kept one eye trained on Albert Payune and noticed the Grand Minister kept an equally close eye on him.

Kathy excused herself from an elderly duke, and Dakota escorted her to the expansive buffet. It was, he thought, the most impressive spread he had ever seen. Each delicacy was a work of art, but Kathy had told him that renowned chefs from around the world had been flown in to prepare the menu. Serving platters brimmed with deviled quail eggs, gingered capon, crab soufflé, tender meats, fresh vegetables and exotic fruits. The dessert tables displayed decadent cakes, parfaits, tortes, tarts and meringues.

They filled their plates and sat beside each other in their designated seats. Kathy sampled a lobster crepe, then looked up and smiled. Their gazes locked in an intense stare, and Dakota knew their minds had connected. Yesterday's erotic admission billowed between them like a warm, sensual cloud. Both still fantasized about being in each other's arms—aroused and naked.

Her tongue darted out to taste the crepe, and he nearly groaned. He wanted to kiss her. Here. Right now. In front of the king and all of his fancily attired court.

But as other guests occupied their table, Dakota reined in his hormones. And while they ate their meal, they engaged in varied conversations.

On occasion Dakota glanced at Payune from across the room and noticed Payune kept stealing glances at the queen.

After dessert and coffee, the king and queen danced the first waltz. Dakota and Kathy stood with other guests, watching the royal couple glide across the floor.

"They look so right together," Kathy said, her voice tinged with sadness.

Dakota frowned. His wife was still upset by the queen's troubled marriage. Or was it the reminder of their own broken vows that she thought of tonight? He sensed this was not the moment to ask her to dance. Instead he suggested they explore the alcoves in the ballroom, and she readily agreed.

The first windowed section held a pair of seventeenth-century Venetian chairs, and the second displayed borders of rose-covered silk and a marble table.

Kathy examined a gilded vase on the table, and Dakota moved closer. "Did you wear your hair like that for me?" he asked, studying the tumbling red tresses she normally struggled to contain. He would not allow her sadness to linger. Not tonight.

She hesitated, then met his gaze, her eyes as illuminating as her gown. "Yes," she said softly.

"Because you knew I would want to run my hands through it?"

"Yes," she whispered again.

He skimmed her cheek. She hadn't reapplied her lipstick. Her lips were moist and slightly parted, just waiting for his. Dare he kiss her now? Inside the palace?

He dropped his hand. He couldn't. There were too many guests milling about, too many foreign dignitaries, dukes and counts, lords and ladies.

"Excuse me. Ma'am? Sir?" a voice said.

Dakota cursed his lack of focus. Someone had managed to approach without his knowledge. And at the very moment he had been debating a kiss, no less. He raised an eyebrow at Kathy. She, too, seemed surprised. Unsure of what to expect, they turned simultaneously.

Prince Eric stood before them. In spite of his regal posture and proper tuxedo, the boy's appearance made Dakota smile. The child's thick black hair rebelled from a slick side part, a cowlick fighting desperately for control. Apparently the young prince had hair as hard to tame as Kathy's.

They responded to the boy as protocol dictated, and Dakota decided Prince Eric owned not an ounce of pretension. He was being groomed to rule an old-world country, but his manner put both Dakota and Kathy at ease.

"Are you a United States Air Force lieutenant?" the boy asked Dakota, clearly wondering why he wasn't in uniform.

"I retired from duty four years ago," Dakota told him.

"Are you a pilot?"

"Yes. Do planes interest you?"

"Yes, and cowboys, too," came the youthful response. "I attend a boarding school in America."

Dakota resisted the urge to slip Kathy a sideways glance. He supposed he looked like a forty-one-year-old cowboy with his rugged skin and hard-earned crow's-feet. His Texas drawl certainly fit the cowboy mold. Dakota didn't have a lot of experience with children, so the last thing he had expected was admiration from an adolescent prince. It boosted his pride with a masculine sort of awe.

"So you like horses, then?"

Prince Eric nodded, his voice a little quieter. "But I prefer a Western saddle to the hunt seat," he said as if the admission might earn him a European scolding. A security officer in the royal service stood a non-intrusive distance away, keeping a careful eye on the boy.

Dakota smiled. He doubted the stoic-faced guard had heard, and even if he had, who would tattle on a future king?

For a moment Dakota thought to invite the child to his ranch. He could teach the young prince about Comanche horsemanship. In Dakota's culture, a boy didn't merely learn to ride. He had to be a trick rider, practice picking up objects while his mount traveled at full speed. And the ten-year-old prince, with his rebellious hair and dark, curious eyes, would make a quick study. European royalty, he thought, with a Comanche soul.

Dakota shook off the notion, realizing he had allowed an unexpected paternal urge to get the best of him. He couldn't extend an invitation to Price Eric, he thought, a twinge of regret constricting his chest. Who would explain his true marital status? Who would tell the child that Kathy no longer lived at the ranch? It was bad enough the young Prince would be burdened by his parents' personal problems. He didn't need to be dragged into Dakota's as well.

After Prince Eric departed, Dakota and Kathy returned to the main ballroom. As they left the charming alcove, Kathy's heartbeat quickened. Heading toward them was Albert Payune, his steely blue eyes focused directly on her.

There was no way to avoid him. Soon they would come face-to-face with the man who had been watching them for most of the night. Did Payune know that Prince Eric had looked upon Dakota with youthful admiration? Or that Dakota had smiled affectionately at the child? The rightful heir to the Asterland throne?

Payne shifted his gaze to Dakota. "Lieutenant Lewis," he said in a formal greeting. "Are you enjoying the ball?"

"Yes, thank you. And you, sir?"

Such stifled pleasantries, Kathy thought, her pulse refusing to relax. How could Dakota stand there looking so calm?

Because it was his job, she reminded herself. Her husband thrived on danger.

"It is a lovely affair," Payune responded in an unemotional tone. He turned to Kathy, trapping her with a cool smile. "Mrs. Lewis, you look simply stunning."

She forced herself to meet those frosty blue eyes. "Thank you."

He held her gaze, and she knew he was testing her, waiting to see if she squirmed. She lifted her chin a notch, even though she feared the pounding of her heart would give her panic away.

"Your husband came to see me the other day," Payune said. "We had quite an interesting chat."

She glanced briefly at Dakota. He didn't come closer, didn't coax or comfort her in any way. But the Grand Minister studied them with keen interest. Assessing their body language, she assumed.

"Yes, he told me," she said. "And I do hope you will consider his offer."

"We shall see. For now, it is much too grand a night to concern ourselves with business." He reached for her hand and brushed his mouth over her knuckles in the same manner he had brushed off her statement. "But I would be honored, Mrs. Lewis, if you would save me a dance."

"Of course." She wanted to snag her hand back and wipe it on her dress. Even his lips were cold.

Dakota moved in with a smile, touching her with sudden familiarity. She did her best not to collapse in his arms.

"My lovely wife promised me a tour of the gardens. Didn't you, darling?"

"Yes, I did. The grounds are breathtaking."

"Do not detain her for too long, Lieutenant." Payune split his cool gaze between them. "I am looking forward to that dance."

The instant Kathy and Dakota stepped outside, she allowed herself a nervous shiver.

"Are you cold?" he asked. "Do you need your jacket?"

"No, I'm fine. The air feels good." She took a deep,

cleansing breath. Already she could smell sweet, earthy scents rising from the flowers. She would draw from their beauty, she thought. Their magic. Surely the palace gardens had resident fairies, little winged creatures who would keep them safe.

They walked arm in arm for a short while, taking the stone path that would eventually lead to the maze. As they came upon the queen's traditional rose garden, he spoke in a hushed tone. Other guests explored the grounds, their voices a distant buzz.

"You did fine, sweetheart."

"He's suspicious of us."

"Of course, he is. I expected as much. He isn't the sort of man who puts his trust in others. Not even those he considers allies."

And that worried her. Payune might accept Dakota's offer, might bring him into the revolution, but her husband would be watched. Maybe too closely.

Before she could ask if he thought they were being followed, Dakota stopped to draw her into his arms. Needing him, she came willingly. He dipped his head and his breath fluttered across her cheek, then brushed her lips.

The kiss was tender and protective, and she welcomed it from deep within her soul. Roses flourished all around them— a gathering of soft, velvety petals—long, sturdy stems and prickly thorns. Beauty and danger, her mind warned.

This man.

This moment.

Their tongues touched lightly, ever so lightly. It was a tease, an awakening. He tasted of Russian vodka. Just a little, she realized, just enough to induce a slow, warm intoxication.

She let the sensation steep her, heat and melt and pull her into a dreamy state. He licked her bare shoulder, grazed it with his teeth. She clung to him, felt a shift in his stance. She inhaled his cologne, wanting to breathe him into her lungs, into her body.

He nuzzled her neck, then lifted his head and brought his face next to hers. "We have to go. We can't stay here."

"I know." Somewhere in the back of her foggy mind, she heard voices. Someone was speaking French. A language as fluid as their kiss.

Although flood lights lit the gardens, shadows danced across their path—dark, leafy shapes—tall, billowy figures. Their feet scraped the stone walk, scattering pebbles. The natural perfume from the roses had disappeared. Beyond them lay an endless carpet of grass, and in the distance a dark, ominous structure.

The maze stood like an ancient castle, ghostly and foreboding. The music from the palace seemed ghostly, too—a lonely waltz drifting into the shadows.

"It looks haunted," Kathy said. And if someone followed, they couldn't be sure. Payune could have sent a tail—a dark figure who blended into the night. There were too many shrubs, too many trees in which to take cover.

They cut across the grass; it was damp and freshly mowed. She felt her shoes sink into the moisture.

The opening of the maze beckoned, and she feared that first step. It would swallow them, and then Dakota would disappear.

They followed the path they had memorized. It went on forever, twists and turns, fake passageways, clever openings. There was enough light to keep from stumbling, but not enough to make her feel safe.

The gazebo surfaced like a mirage, but it, too, seemed haunted. The swing rocked on its own, just a little, just enough to frighten her. A spray of flowers grew from the soil—blooms too unusual and too exotic to name. Nothing felt familiar. Nothing felt right.

The night had eyes, she thought.

Dakota took her hand and guided her into a corner—a tall, rectangular shape that led to another geometric cove.

And then his mouth came down on hers.

Hard.

So hard she locked her knees to keep herself from falling. There was no time to think, no time to dwell on ghosts and swings and heady-scented flowers. His hands, those big, powerful hands circled her waist and pulled her flush against him.

This was no phantom lover, no figment of her imagination. He was real, solid, built of bronzed flesh and unyielding bones. She explored the breadth of his shoulders, the tapering of his waist, the muscles that jumped in his stomach.

And while arousal flooded her system, he played with the zipper on her dress, sliding it down, then back up again—cupping her bottom, pressing heat against heat.

She heard sounds. Her sigh. His low growl. The slice of her zipper.

He delved into her hair, and she felt it fall into his hands, tumble over his wrists and down his arms.

He kissed her, over and over, sipping and tasting. Her nipples tingled against the silk of her bra, the satin of her dress.

They made love through their clothes, she thought. There was no other way to describe the sleek, sliding motion. The pressure building upon need. The hot, fumbling strokes.

But they didn't have long. It would end too soon—this glorious, wicked sensation. And it wasn't enough, not nearly enough.

He gentled the kiss, then drew back to look at her, his breathing a series of husky pants. Moonlight slashed across his face—the razor edge of his cheekbones, the sensual shape of his lips, the hard, smooth line of his jaw.

"I wish I could take you. Here. Right now."

She understood, and the thought made her dizzy. He wanted to lift her dress, remove her panties, untuck his shirt, open his trousers.

Suddenly she didn't care if the night had eyes. She could almost feel him moving deep inside her, each powerful thrust urging them to completion. "Then stay with me," she whispered.

He rubbed his forehead across hers, his voice quiet—broken words only they could hear. "I can't. You know I can't."

Yes, she knew. But the fear had returned, and she didn't want to lose him. It was always the same fear, the one that had surfaced soon after she'd married him. He would go away and never come back.

Don't do this to me, she wanted to say. Don't make me remember why I can't be your wife. Not now. Not while I'm here in your arms.

"Close your eyes," he told her.

She did as he asked, and he carried her to the connecting cove. As her feet touched the ground, he kissed her. A touch that fluttered across her lips like the elusive wings of a butterfly.

She could still smell the woodsy scent of his cologne, but when she opened her eyes, she looked into the shadowy face of a stranger. Dakota was gone, and in his place stood the man called Thunder.

Payune's estate wasn't far from the palace, and Thunder had left everything Dakota needed, including a vehicle that took him to a grassy field laden with foliage. Dakota parked between two gnarled old trees, then brought the night optics to his eyes. He could see the stone wall that surrounded the Grand Minister's estate. He had studied the floor plan of the sprawling estate, and he knew the home contained three safes. The necklace could be in any one of them, but he was banking on the one located in the master suite.

Dakota adjusted his gloves. He had already slipped on a pair of dark coveralls and changed his shoes. There was nothing left to do but switch the necklaces and return to Kathy's waiting arms.

What would happen to Kathy if he foiled this mission? Dakota started across the field, his mind suddenly troubled. Thunder would take care of her. The other man had given his word.

A burst of masculine rivalry surged through his veins like a charge of angry adrenaline. Yeah, that was all he needed. A guy who looked like himself taking care of his wife.

His face shielded by a ski mask, Dakota scaled the wall, grateful Payune wasn't a fan of guard dogs. Or dogs in general. All Dakota had to think about was the household staff, and a skeletal crew at that. Apparently Payune didn't trust employees of the royal service any more than he trusted a Doberman or a rottweiler not to turn on him. But then Payune was a man who had plenty to hide, and people as well as dogs could usually smell a rat. Especially if they lived under the same roof with one.

Taking to the shadows, Dakota disengaged the alarm, a tedious task of stripping and rearranging wires. He did the same with the phone lines, knowing he would have to reverse the process after he switched the necklaces.

Dodging flood lights and a security camera, he ascended the terrace like a mountain climber claiming Mount Everest, then stood beside the door that led to the master suite, his back to a stone wall.

Get in and get out, he told himself. Kathy was waiting.

Frowning, he picked the lock. That's right. Kathy waited in the maze, in a dark, cozy corner with Thunder—an Apache with the heart of a rogue and a smile to match. Women loved the hell out of that guy. And Dakota trusted him. Until now.

Payune's private suite came into view, but Dakota didn't waste time assessing the man's ostentatious taste in art and antiques. There were three sets of connecting rooms. He turned to the wall that contained the built-in safe and grinned. This was too easy—a scene from an outdated television show. An aristocratic portrait with a stolen necklace behind it.

He went to work on the safe and what he didn't find had him cursing under his breath. That out-dated television script had just thrown him a Hollywood curve ball. There wasn't a ruby in sight.

The library or the office? he asked himself. Which safe was it in? He checked his watch and thought about Kathy. With Thunder.

He slipped out of Payune's suite and took up residence in an unlit corner of the hallway. The servants' quarters were in the back of the house, and he could only hope the household staff had tucked themselves in for the night. And if not, he had already mapped out every escape route imaginable.

The stairs descended in a circular motion, a slick polished

banister guiding the way. He took each step soundlessly. But as he made his way toward the library, he spotted a flood of light streaking beneath the kitchen door. Not a security light like some of the others burning throughout the estate. This bright flash said that someone was working in there.

His senses went into full alert. Freshly baked bread. A pot of simmering soup. The contented hum of a plump, elderly cook.

Footsteps sounded. Foreign voices spoke. Maids, two of them. He stood like a masked statue, his body molded to the side of an antique hutch taller and wider than himself. The women entered the kitchen, and he heard feminine chatter and bowls clanking. Apparently the cook had prepared a late-night meal.

When the rat is away, Dakota thought, his mouth splitting into a grin—the household staff will gossip and play.

A push of pure adrenaline led him into the library. He went right to his mark, pulled out the false front on a bookshelf and uncovered the safe.

The rubies glittered like blood, and a surge of excitement shot straight to his groin. With his mind on his wife, he slipped the necklace into a pouch, leaving the fake for Payune.

Years of experience kept Dakota on track, even though Kathy occupied his thoughts. He completed the job and returned to the palace grounds. With a pounding heart, he followed the twists and turns in the maze, then stopped when he saw them.

Kathy and Thunder.

They stood near the gazebo, leaning toward each other, their shadowed faces much too close. Thunder could have been him, Dakota thought. No one would suspect that the man gazing into Kathy's eyes was an imposter. He looked like her husband.

Her lover.

A knot of jealousy twisted Dakota's gut. He mimicked the caw of a raven, signaling his return—a call Thunder would recognize.

The other man leaned a little closer to Kathy, then took her hand and guided her toward the section of the maze where Dakota waited. Kathy didn't seem aware of what was happening, but Dakota knew she couldn't see him, not when a tall, dark shrub stood between them.

"I'll be right back," Thunder whispered as he moved away from her.

Like hell you will, Dakota thought, even though he knew Thunder didn't intend to keep his word.

A moment later, the two men came face-to-face, but neither dared speak. Dakota handed over the pouch containing the necklace, and Thunder grinned before he stole into the night, letting Dakota know he had enjoyed every minute of his assignment.

Wonderful. His wife and the guy who had taken a bullet for him. How was that for an equation?

Dakota slipped around the hedge and, in spite of the darkness, Kathy recognized him instantly. She threw her arms around his neck and practically melted in his arms.

He stroked her hair and smiled. Apparently he had been missed.

Their mouths came together then, more in relief than passion, but an overwhelming pleasure squeezed his heart. At that mind-spinning moment, he felt loved.

Beautifully, thoroughly loved. An illusion, maybe. But a damn good one.

"We can't stay," he whispered as they came up for air. "We have to go back." The job had taken longer than he'd expected, and they couldn't afford to arouse Payune's suspicion anymore than they already had.

"I know," she responded, stroking his face as though his features might disappear if she didn't touch him.

They walked back to the palace, but before they re-entered the ballroom, Kathy stopped and let out a breath. "Do I look a mess?"

He smiled. Her hair fell about her shoulders in gorgeous disarray and her cheeks as well as her lips were flushed. "You look thoroughly kissed, sweetheart."

She didn't return his smile. "I have to freshen up before anyone sees me." She glanced down at her shoes. "Oh, goodness. They have grass stains."

He suppressed an amused grin. Her shoes were green to begin with, an emerald satin that matched her dress. "I don't think anyone will notice. But I'll escort you to the nearest powder room, so you can get yourself together. Okay?"

"Thank you."

"Kathy?" He took her hand. "Afterward, will you dance with me?"

She went stiff, her hand suddenly cold. "I promised *him* a dance."

And Payune would be waiting, Dakota thought. "Don't worry, you'll get through it. And if he tries to monopolize your time, I'll cut in." Dakota wanted to hold her, just once more. In spite of the sexy things they had said to each other earlier, he knew they wouldn't be sharing the same bed tonight. Stars still lit up the sky and flowers still scented the air, but the moment had passed.

"What am I supposed to say if he asks where we've been? We've been gone a long time, Dakota."

He guided her to the door. "Just tell him we got lost in the maze." It was, he thought, as close to the truth as they could admit. Even to themselves.

Five

Two days after the ball, Dakota entered Albert Payune's home, an invitation extended by a phone call early that morning. The butler escorted him to the parlor, and Payune told the servant not to disturb him. Besides Payune, there were three other men already in the room. Dakota recognized all of them. Two were low-level Asterland cabinet members—willing participants in the impending revolution, he assumed.

And the third?

Dakota locked gazes with the average-looking man. He could have been anyone's neighbor, European or American. With his wavy brown hair and relaxed stance, he didn't appear to have a sinister bone in his body. Dakota knew otherwise. Mark Delray, as he had just been formally introduced, was a hired assassin. They had never met before, but Dakota had seen Mark's photograph in a top-secret military file. Different name, but that average, nice-guy face was one he wasn't likely to forget.

Someone was going to be murdered. Today, tomorrow or

possibly the day after. Soon, he thought, the assassin would
strike soon. Dakota glanced around the room and hoped to
hell he wasn't the intended recipient of Mark Delray's hit.

Kathy had practically worn a hole in the carpet. What was
taking so long? Where was Dakota? She peered out the window. Dusk had begun to settle in the sky. A bright orange
sun was setting, a silvery moon hiding somewhere, waiting
to take its place.

Feeling claustrophobic, she headed out the front door and
down the scattered-stone walkway until she reached the
grassy cliffs. She needed to breathe, needed to feel the wind
on her face.

There was no one to call, no one to spill her worries to.
How long could a meeting with Payune take? Dakota had left
six hours ago.

Six hours. Six days. At the moment she couldn't distin-
guish the difference. All she knew was that he hadn't returned, and she feared for his safety.

Thunder would contact her if there was trouble. She tugged
on an errant strand of hair as it fell free from its pinned coif-
fure. What if Thunder didn't know Dakota was in trouble.
What then?

She stared out at the hilly terrain. The beauty mocked her
mood. The sky was ablaze with a fiery glow and wildflowers
dotted the hills with a lavender hue.

She spotted a familiar SUV in the distance, a white Mer-
cedes ML moving up the winding road. "Thank you, God,"
she whispered.

Dakota parked the vehicle, and she stood watching him,
the wind playing havoc with her hair. She couldn't run to
him, no matter how much she wanted to. If she took that first
step, she would probably burst into tears and cry in his arms,
shake uncontrollably and kiss him senseless.

So she waited instead, her feet bare, the hem of a pale blue
dress billowing in the breeze, her heart as fiery as the setting
sun. Suddenly she wanted to kiss him, taste and tug and pull
him to the ground. She wanted to feel those muscles bunch

beneath her hands, hold him and never let go. He was safe. He was safe.

He exited the car, then caught sight of her. For a moment he stood motionless, watching the way she watched him. And then he smiled, a flash of white in that dark handsome face.

He came toward her, then stopped just shy of touching. "It's over," he said. "Or it will be in the morning."

"Over?"

"Payune and the others will be arrested tomorrow. I found what I needed to know and passed the information to Thunder."

"And Thunder contacted the Royal Police?"

Dakota nodded. "Payune is expecting the money tomorrow, but that's not what he's going to get."

Kathy released a sigh of relief. If her feet weren't planted so firmly in the grass, she might have lost her footing and toppled over. "You did it."

"We did it," he corrected gently. "I couldn't have pulled this off without you."

She blinked back a collection of tears. The sun had disappeared, but the sky was still a haven of color. Magenta streaks blazed through slashes of orange and beams of midnight blue. It was beautiful, and so was he—this tall, powerful man.

"Kathy?"

"Hmmm?"

"They were going to kill the king."

Her heart went still, much too still. But rather than respond in a frightened voice, she waited for Dakota to continue. "It wasn't Payune's original plan. But when he heard that the royal marriage was in trouble, he got this insane brainstorm."

Dakota pulled a hand through his hair, spiking the thick, ebony strands. "Payune tried to convince me that the king was emotionally disturbed, just like Prince Ivan."

Kathy's heart was no longer still, it pounded with a hard thump. "They were going to murder King Bertram and make it look like a suicide."

"That's right. And in Payune's warped mind, Queen Nicole would have eventually turned to him for solace. Of course Payune didn't admit to any of this outright, but one of the other cabinet members got my attention on the sly."

"How?" she asked, picturing Dakota in that risky situation.

"He was pouring drinks for everyone. And when he handed mine over, he whispered, 'follow me.' I knew he meant after the meeting. At first I was concerned that I was being set up for a hit. But then, something—instinct, I guess—told me he was going to make some sort of confession." Kathy fought a shiver, and Dakota continued. "So after the meeting I followed him to a deserted road."

"And he told you about Payune's plan?"

"Yes, he did. And he's willing to cooperate with the Royal Police. He never expected this to come down to murder, but he didn't know how to approach the police without arousing Payune's suspicion."

Kathy battled another chill, realizing how often Dakota had been exposed to dangerous situations. "How did this cabinet member know you were out to get Payune?"

"He didn't. He just figured an American businessman wouldn't want to be implicated in the assassination of a king."

She tipped her head and looked up at the sky, then back at Dakota. "I'm so glad it's over."

"Me, too."

They stood staring at each other, and she nearly lost her breath. "I'm going to miss this cottage." And she would miss him—those piercing black eyes and that Comanche smile.

"It is kind of magical." He moved closer, brushing his body against hers, his lips just a heartbeat away.

A pounding, drumming heartbeat.

He lowered his head, and she closed her eyes. There was no time to think, to rationalize. There was only Dakota's mouth covering hers.

He tasted as clean as the elements, as spicy as the scent of his cologne. She stood on her toes and clung to him. Heat burned throughout her body, making her breath catch in her throat. She arched to feel as much of him as she could, but it wasn't enough.

While he kissed her, she tugged his shirt from his trousers, then unbuttoned it, searching for muscle and male flesh. The wind snapped the tails of the fabric, pulling it away from his chest. She grazed him with her nails, and he shifted his hips and deepened the kiss.

His hands were suddenly everywhere, all over her, sliding and roaming. He went after the front of her dress, popping buttons as he did. Dragging his lips down the column of her neck, he unhooked her bra. Kathy moaned and bit his shoulder. Dakota tongued her nipple.

She held him against her breast and watched him suckle. A blade of moonlight glinted off his hair, and she realized dusk had slipped into darkness. Her bra remained slack, falling against her body.

No, there was no time to think. No time to care about anything but how he made her feel. She had become part of this enchanted world—the cliffs and the trees and the ocean crashing below. She pictured the waves rising and swelling, bathing the rocks in crystalline sheets. Just as Dakota bathed her—with his mouth, his tongue.

She buried her hands in his hair while he licked, then pulled on those short spiky strands as he closed his teeth around her. It was gentle. It was rough. An ache that brought both pleasure and pain.

When he stepped back to look at her, a light breeze blew across her nipples, chilling them.

"Tell me you want more," he said.

Her breath rushed out of her lungs. "I do." She wanted everything. Every touch, every kiss, every slick, hot sensation he could give her. "I want more."

As he pushed her dress from her shoulders, Kathy felt it pool at her feet in a flutter of pale-blue lace.

Their gazes locked in a magnetic pull. His eyes were black against the night, dark and compelling. And his face, so close to hers, was hard and smooth and mildly abrasive. She stroked his skin, memorizing him beneath the stars.

He didn't remove her panties. Instead he skimmed her

tummy, then slid his hand under the elastic. She rocked against his hand, and he stroked—a gentle, rhythmic pressure.

He pushed a finger deep inside, and she gasped. More. Yes, she wanted more. He kissed her, took her mouth while he made her unbearably wet.

She tasted desire in his kiss, felt it blaze like a neon moon. She gripped his shoulders and lost herself in his touch—his hand moving between her thighs, those long, callused fingers teasing and arousing.

Deeper.

Wetter.

"Let it happen," he whispered.

She had no choice. The wind rushed through her hair, spilling pieces over her shoulders and down her arms. One strand adhered itself to her nipple, to the moisture he had made. His fingers surged into her with exquisite force. Desperate, she kissed him so hard, they both gasped for air.

Need clawed like talons, and she rubbed against his hand—against the pressure, the friction, the fire she couldn't control.

And then suddenly the world stilled, and there was nothing but the sound of her release. She heard it rip from her throat and echo into the night before she closed her eyes and let herself tumble.

Kathy collapsed in his arms, so Dakota held her in a soft, quiet moment. The moon sent fiery streaks through her hair, and her skin glowed with a passionate sheen. She was beautiful. So beautiful. Bathed in the afterglow of the climax he had given her.

He brushed her cheek, and she made a kittenish sound. She was still dazed, still caught between silk and sensation. He ran his hands down the sides of her body, down the long, lithe curves. Her tummy was flat, her hips lean yet womanly, her breasts full, nipples taut and aroused.

He was aroused, too. So damn aroused.

His shirt flapped in the wind, and he wondered if she was cold. She wore nothing but a pair of lace panties. Blue lace and smooth, creamy skin.

"I'm taking you inside." He swept her into his arms, and she clung to him, her hair falling free from its confinement. It spilled over her shoulders like a scarlet ribbon, reminding him of Christmas and birthdays and all the holidays he had missed holding her.

Tonight they would make up for lost time. Tonight, he thought, carrying her to the master bedroom, they would make love.

He placed her on the bed and turned on a lamp. An amber bulb lit the room, illuminating with a soft glow. There were fresh flowers on the nightstand, and he knew she had picked them. They were wild, the same lavender blooms that dotted the cliffs. Everything in the room was decidedly feminine—pillows the color of champagne, window sheers trimmed in lace, a quilt as silky as her skin.

It made him feel erotic, a little forbidden—a man stealing into a lady's chamber at night.

Oh, yes, he thought, as he unbuckled his belt, this cottage was haunted. A sexual haunting he had no will to stop.

"Let me touch you," she said.

"Go ahead," he challenged, his shirt gone, belt undone, trousers unzipped. "Touch as much as you want. Wherever you want."

Painfully aroused, he stood before her while she sat on the edge of the bed and looked up at him. She skimmed his belly, gently abrading him with her nails. And then she leaned forward and pressed her mouth to the scar just below his navel.

His stomach was corrugated with muscles, and each and every one of them jumped, sending a cool, clean shiver straight to his groin.

Damn it. He closed his eyes, then opened them, realizing they had forgotten something. One simple, important little thing.

"I didn't bring any protection." Three years of celibacy had left him without a reason to think about it. Until now. "Tell me we can risk it." They had taken risks before. But Kathy knew her own body, knew when it was safe.

"I..." Something flashed in her eyes. Pain? Sadness? He couldn't be sure, wasn't certain if he wanted to know. Suddenly their emotions were too close to the edge. They were half naked, looking into each other's eyes, stripping each other's souls.

He skimmed her cheek. "Kathy?"

Her breath hitched. "I want you to love me."

"Then I will."

He discarded his boots and shed his belt, then lowered himself to the bed. She reached for his trousers, and together they battled to remove them.

Soon his pants landed at the foot of the bed along with his briefs. She still wore those pale blue panties, so he slipped them off, tugging the lace from her hips.

The sheets smelled sweet, like Kathy, like fresh-picked berries on a summer morning. He imagined living there, in this bed, with her by his side.

They could feed on each other, sustain themselves with sex. Luscious, wild strawberry-scented sex. It was an insane notion, but it made him smile.

And then she reached between their bodies, and every coherent thought slipped from his mind. He surged hot and greedy into her palm, and she closed her fingers around him.

His pulse pounded. He wanted to slam into her, take her as hard and fast as he could. Yet he wanted to savor and touch and kiss and make the urgency last.

Pinning her to the bed, he cuffed her wrists with his hands. Her hair was everywhere, a mass of scarlet ribbon tangling over her shoulders, down her arms, across the pillow. One silky wave curled around one taut, rosy nipple. She was his fantasy. She had always been his ideal, and he had wanted her from the first moment he had seen her.

She looked up at him, seducing him with those exotic green eyes. She must have been a cat in another life, he thought. A lean, leggy creature with claws.

She struggled against his restraint, rising to nuzzle his chest, purring like the feline he imagined her to be.

He smiled and held her down again. Hot and restless, she moved beneath him, challenging him to take her, to make her wet and slick and quivering with lust.

Dakota nearly lost his mind. Releasing her wrists, he slid down her body, over those smooth, feline curves. Placing his mouth against her, he kissed between her thighs. Kissed and licked while she bucked and made throaty little sounds.

He could hear the wind outside, knew it had picked up speed. The same speed as the rhythm of his heart. The beating, the pounding, the rush of excitement.

He tasted her release, felt her orgasm rise and swell, but it still wasn't enough. Not nearly enough.

He needed more. So much more.

Dakota rose above her, then entered her with a deep, sensual stroke. She raised her hips, and together they moved in unison—lovers who relished the pleasure, the warmth, the familiarity of each other.

They couldn't stop kissing, touching, feeling—giving sensation, taking it back.

They rolled over the bed until she straddled him, rode him while he watched. Her hair fell forward, a portion of it still pinned, the rest tangling over her body like fiery vines. She was a goddess, he thought, an enchantress, a mermaid from the sea, a siren from the sky. She was everything he had ever wanted in a lover.

He couldn't think about missing her because she was here, riding him, milking his body with hers. Heat shot through his belly and blazed through his loins, begging for a release. Begging for the strength to hold on. Just one more minute, one more warm, wet spiraling second.

She grasped his hands, locked on and held. He watched her, his vision blurred, his need edgy. And when that last second spun out of control, he threw back his head and let himself fall.

Hours later Dakota opened his eyes, trapped between waking and sleeping. The room was dark, not pitch black, but still too dark to focus. Someone touched him. A hand in his hair, fingertips skimming his shoulder.

He didn't stir. Instead he wondered if he dreamed, if he wasn't awake at all. He slept alone each night, yet there was a woman beside him. The lotion scent of her skin drifted to his nostrils, melding with the lusty lingering of sex.

Kathy. His mind came awake, and his body responded. He grew hard and achy between his thighs—the kind of pressure a woman could relieve. But not just any woman. He wanted his wife.

He turned, shifting in her direction, and her breath caught. He could see her shadow—the outline of a heavenly body with tumbling hair.

"I thought you were asleep," she said.

"I was." He squinted to bring her into focus, but she was still ghostlike. It was the cottage, he thought. The haunting. "You don't have to stop touching me."

"I stayed awake because I wanted you again." She slid down beside him, her leg brushing his. "Before morning."

He struggled to make sense of her words. If she wanted him she could have him now and in the daylight. "We won't turn into pumpkins. Or whatever happens in fairy tales."

"Maybe we will." She ran her hands down the front of his body, over the planes and ridges, muscles that formed his stomach. "Maybe tonight is just a fairy tale."

A tightness, a pain constricted his heart. He understood why she had remained awake. Tomorrow their loving would end. She wasn't offering to come back to him, to become a part of his life again.

What they had was now. His haunting. The darkness that shielded their past and kept them from a future.

He should have turned away, but he couldn't. If this moment was all they had, then he'd take it.

He reached for her, and she moved into his arms. They kissed and then caressed, their hands slipping into a languid rhythm. It was like dancing on a wave, floating on the edge of a dream. Yes, he thought. She was a mermaid, a goddess of the sea. And he couldn't keep her. Nor would he try.

After tonight, he would let her go.

"Kathy," he whispered her name, and she lifted her hips to accept his penetration. His deep, warm strokes.

There were no urgent thrusts. No groping or fumbling. No torn clothes or breathy pants. This was quiet, gentle loving—a joining that came from the heart.

And one Dakota would never forget.

Two days later Kathy held a gold vase, a gift from Queen Nicole and King Bertram. It was truly over. Albert Payune, the other revolutionists and the hired assassin were in jail. The cabinet member who had cooperated with the police would receive a lesser sentence for exposing the murder plot.

She studied the sparkling sapphire imbedded in the vase. King Bertram was a gracious man. Both he and the queen had thanked Dakota and Kathy personally, offering a valuable gift in honor and gratitude. The Asterland government had also promised that Payune would not be able to spread the word that the Lone Star jewels actually existed. The legend would be protected.

"Kathy?"

She turned to the sound of Dakota's voice. He hadn't stepped foot in the master bedroom since the night they'd made love. She had awakened that morning to find him gone. Later she'd discovered he'd left the cottage to roam the hills, then tie up the loose ends of their mission.

"Have you finished packing?" he asked.

"No, but I'm nearly done." She tried to avoid his gaze, but couldn't quite manage. Those Comanche eyes held her captive, trapping her in deep, dark emotion.

"It's beautiful, isn't it?" He motioned to the vase. "Kind of an unusual shape, though."

Should she tell him? Kathy wondered. Tell him why her vase had a curved indentation and his rounded on one side? Apparently he hadn't examined them closely enough to make the connection. "They're a set."

He blinked. "What?"

"The vases."

He reached for the jeweled object, a small frown creasing his brow. She watched as he ran his hand over the gold, following the shape. "It means something, doesn't it? Something significant?"

Kathy released a quiet breath. "They represent love. They're very old and valuable. There aren't that many in existence, and in Asterland when they're given as a gift, they're always given to a couple, sometimes on their wedding day."

Kathy glanced down at her hand and realized she still wore her wedding ring, the diamonds and emeralds Dakota had given her. She noticed Dakota still wore his, too. But he had chosen white gold and onyx. A design that didn't resemble a wedding band—a ring that rarely interfered with his undercover work. It was a piece of jewelry that looked natural on an Indian man, whether he wore it on his left hand or switched it to his right.

"Love." Dakota cleared his throat as if to clear away a sudden huskiness. The discomfort in his eyes wasn't hard to miss. "You didn't tell the queen about our cover, did you? She thinks we've reconciled. That we're making a fresh start in our marriage."

"I didn't have the opportunity to tell her." Kathy folded a blouse and placed it in her suitcase, giving herself something to do. "And after she and the king gave us the vases, it seemed too late. The gesture had already been made."

Shifting the object in question, Dakota's frown deepened. "Mine fits against yours." He lifted his gaze. "Like our bodies."

"I think that's the idea." She knew her voice sounded rigid, but she couldn't relax her throat. He had practically abandoned her after they'd made love. But then what had she expected? For him to say that he would retire for good? That their marriage was more important than the next mission? Sex wouldn't change that, no matter how incredible it had been.

To ease some of the tension building in the room, she took the vase and placed it on the bed. "I don't think the symbolism was meant just for us. I think the gift was also the queen's way of saying that she and the king are trying to work through their differences.'' And for that, Kathy was deeply relieved. Not only did the monarchs truly love each other, they had a child to consider—a ten-year-old boy.

"That's good.'' Dakota stood with impeccable posture, a military stance that fit his tall, broad stature. ''They're a nice family,'' he said, revealing an affection for Prince Eric that mirrored her own.

"Yes, they are.''

Telling herself not to dwell on dark-eyed children, she glanced at the wilting wildflowers on the nightstand and realized the extent of her loneliness. She hadn't been in the mood to walk the cliffs, enjoy the scent of the ocean or pick lavender flowers. All of those pleasures reminded her too much of Dakota. Even the garden was a sad reminder. Making wishes and imagining fairies seemed foolish now.

"Are you going back to D.C.?''

She looked up. "No, I'm not. I'm leaving the Bureau.''

"For good?''

"Yes. I gave my notice before we came here.'' A decision that had been a long time coming.

Dakota hooked his thumbs in his jeans, suddenly looking more like a cowboy than a retired air force officer. Why hadn't she noticed his Wranglers and embroidered Western shirt before? His lizard-skin boots and tooled leather belt? He had well-dressed Texan written all over him.

Kathy closed her suitcase. Maybe she hadn't wanted to notice. Maybe she found the image just a bit too sexy.

"So what are you going to do?'' he asked.

"Head up a satellite office for my parents' business.'' Her grandfather had founded a successful import/export company. Kathy's family had been living abroad for as long as she could remember. So joining the Foreign Service had seemed like a natural step. But now she wanted to live in the States, someplace other than the Capitol.

"So where are you going to set up shop, so to speak?''

She lifted her chin. "In Royal.''

His jaw nearly dropped. "You mean Texas? Where I live?"

She narrowed her eyes. "As you may recall, I lived there once, too." After Dakota had retired from the air force, Kathy had taken an extended leave of absence from the Foreign Service, hoping for a quiet, domestic life at the ranch, one Dakota had never given her. In spite of his retirement, the dangerous missions continued. "I like Royal. I have friends there."

"Of course you do." He softened his voice. "So you've rented an apartment already?"

"No, but I intend to. I've already arranged for a moving company to ship my belongings to Royal."

"Oh."

They stood in awkward silence after that, Dakota staring at his boots and Kathy reorganizing cosmetics in her makeup bag, hoping to look busy enough for him to just leave her be.

Finally he lifted his gaze and broke through the quiet. "You're welcome to stay with me. You know, just until you find a place."

Her heart leaped forward with a hard thump. "Do you think that's wise?"

"Why wouldn't it be?" he responded a bit too easily. "Since we've already gotten each other out of our systems, it just might be possible for us to be friends. There's certainly no harm in trying."

Gotten each other out of our systems. Maybe Dakota was right. Maybe it was time to accept him as a friend. She had lived in limbo long enough. And so had he. They both needed to come to terms with their broken marriage and move on with their lives.

"Thank you." She forced a casual smile. "I promise I won't wear out my welcome."

"Don't worry about it." He returned her smile, then offered to carry her suitcase out to the car. This tall, gorgeous man who still made her heart beat much too fast.

Six

Dakota was back in Texas and wondering if he'd gone crazy. He'd left Asterland behind, but he'd brought Kathy with him—to the ranch, the house they'd once shared. She was in the guest room he'd offered, and she'd been holed up in there all day.

He squared his shoulders and headed in the direction of her room. They couldn't hide from each other. Both had agreed to embrace friendship.

He knocked, then stepped back a little. Embracing friendship wasn't the same as embracing each other.

She opened the door, and he cursed a sudden, unwelcome jolt of lust. Her hair, damp from a late-day shower, fell loose about her shoulders. And she wasn't wearing a bra. He could see the faint outline of her breasts through a printed cotton dress.

"Hi," she said.

"Hi." Dumbstruck, he couldn't think of another thing to say. Why had he gone to her room? What had he hoped to accomplish?

"Are you settled in all right?"

"Yes. Thank you."

So polite, he thought, so proper. Even with damp hair and no bra. "Are you hungry? It's lunchtime," he added hastily. Her nipples were erect, poking against the flowers on her dress.

She tucked a lock of wet hair behind her ear. He could smell her shampoo. "Are you fixing lunch? Or are you going out?" she asked.

"I thought I'd fix something here. Mrs. Miller did some shopping for me this morning." And he didn't have the slightest idea what to make. Lunch had been an afterthought, just something to talk about.

Kathy let the door fall open. Behind her Dakota could see the unmade bed. The sheets probably smelled like strawberries by now, like her hair and her skin.

"So Mrs. Miller still works for you?"

He pulled his eyes away from the bed. "Yes, and she hasn't changed a bit."

Kathy smiled. "Same starched gray hair, same white uniform, same squeaky white shoes?"

"That's her." And the housekeeper's non-meddling, get-the-job done personality suited him just fine.

"Can you give me a few minutes before lunch? I still have to dry my hair."

"Sure. No problem."

He made his way to the kitchen, opened the refrigerator and rummaged through the groceries. What in the hell had possessed him to invite Kathy to stay with him? Self torture? He hadn't gotten her out of his system. Not by a long shot.

Forcing himself to concentrate on food, Dakota decided on grilled cheese sandwiches and a black bean salad. The salad took a lot of dicing and slicing, but it contained some of his favorite ingredients: bell and jalapeño peppers, onions, cilantro, parsley and Roma tomatoes.

Kathy entered the kitchen just as he poured the Southwestern mixture over a bed of lettuce and garnished it with lime wedges.

"I should have known you would make something spicy."

He glanced up to acknowledge her, and when she turned toward the dining room, he noticed her dress was one of those great little backless numbers. Talk about spicy. "You know me. A creature of habit." Hot food and sleek redheads. His tastes would never change.

While she took it upon herself to set the table, he grilled the sandwiches. Maybe spending time together at the cottage had made things easier on them. They fell into a domestic pattern as if it were routine. But then, it used to be. They had always shared kitchen duties.

They sat across from each other at an early Texas table scarred with over a century of wear. It suited Dakota's lifestyle as well as the rugged surroundings. His home wasn't a showcase for wealthy living, nor was it actually a working ranch. He owned horses because they gave him pleasure and steers because he enjoyed hosting an occasional Friday-night jackpot for amateur cowboys. And since his ranch hands tended to the animals as nonintrusively as Mrs. Miller tended to the house, he was able to protect his personal life. No one gossiped about Dakota Lewis. Not anymore. He had worked damn hard to be regarded as something other than a billionaire's half-breed, bastard son. High society, he knew, wasn't always kind.

He looked across the table at Kathy. She ate the food he'd prepared, even scooped a diced jalepeño into her mouth. In spite of the disciplined, air force officer image he'd carved out for himself, she used to tell him that he liked everything hot and fast, that he lived on pure heat and adrenaline.

Dakota watched her sip a frothy glass of milk. As if Miss proper-and-pretty had room to talk. The woman was downright wicked in bed, and the stuffy society types she'd dated before him hadn't satisfied her need for hot, fast sex.

"When is Mrs. Miller coming back?" Kathy asked.

Dakota blinked. Answering a question about his no-nonsense housekeeper while he had been thinking about hot-and-fast sex with his gorgeous wife wasn't an easy transition for his male brain to make.

"Wednesday afternoon." He reached for his coffee, hoping the caffeine would snap his senses back in order. "Her schedule hasn't changed." The older lady didn't live at the ranch. Instead she worked four days a week, whether Dakota was home or away on an assignment.

Kathy lifted her napkin. "Does she know I'm here?"

"Yes, I told her."

"So she understands it's just a temporary stay?"

He tried not to frown. "Yes." It hadn't been easy telling the housekeeper that his wife was sleeping in one of the guest rooms. His pride, he supposed, along with his heart, had taken a bruising just saying the words out loud. "There won't be any misunderstandings." Nor would he pressure Kathy about why she had left in the first place. Eventually he would ask, but for now he would do his best to concentrate on friendship.

Dakota tilted his head, pushing the brim of his Stetson back a notch. West Texas was a sight to behold, even before the break of dawn. The moon peeked through a menagerie of clouds as they moved across a vast, deep-blue sky.

Dakota turned toward Ben Rassad. "Do you paint?" he asked, wondering how someone would go about capturing a crescent moon or a shifting cloud.

"No," the sheikh answered. "But I appreciate those who do."

Ben, too, seemed mesmerized by the sky. But Dakota supposed once a man lived in Texas, there was no turning back. The Lone Star state flowed through his veins, whether he was an Amythrarian sheikh or a Comanche pilot.

"The others should be here soon," Dakota said, focusing on their purpose. The Texas Cattleman's Club didn't normally hold pre-dawn meetings in the middle of a park, but this meeting was probably the most significant gathering this group would ever have. The recovered Lone Star jewels would be hidden on this brisk May morning. The private park, which housed the Cattleman's Club and an old adobe mission, also offered acres of greenery. Neither the exclusive gentlemen's club nor the historic mission was visible from the spot they had chosen, but the park, with its tree-lined paths and seasonal blooms, was as familiar to Dakota as his own home.

"Tex is waiting," Ben noted.

Dakota smiled. In 1901, Tex Langley had founded the Texas Cattleman's Club, and these days the rugged oil baron stood in the form of a prestigious bronze statue erected just a few feet away.

Dr. Justin Webb and Matt Walker arrived together. And like Dakota, both the surgeon and the horse breeder sported Western hats and boots. Minutes later diplomat Aaron Black joined the group, and the men greeted each other quietly.

Other than nesting birds and curious squirrels, there wasn't a sign of life seen or heard within miles. The gated park was deserted, and the road that led to it as dark as the night sky.

"So this is it," Matt said, studying the designated location.

Dakota nodded. A small reflecting pool was under construction. The forms had already been set and the rebar was in place, leaving rows of soil between round metal rods. All they had to do was bury the tiny, sealed case containing the priceless gems and wait for the unsuspecting contractors to arrive to pour the concrete.

While the other men stood in the shadows, Dakota dug a deep, narrow hole with a small camper shovel, and Matt placed the airtight case inside. Their only light was a solitary beam from a flashlight. Even the moon respected their silent task, its crescent shape slipping behind a cluster of trees.

The jewels had been originally hidden in a secret passageway in the old mission, and securing them this time seemed simple by comparison. But Dakota knew what each man had risked in an effort to recover the gems. Their lives, as well as those of the women they loved, had been laden with danger. The triumphant moment belonged to all of them.

Dakota stepped away from the burial site. The moon had resurfaced, bathing the ground with a soft silver glow. It seemed fitting somehow—ceremonial to a Comanche who believed Mother Earth provided all things sacred.

Leadership. Justice. Peace. Those three words shone in the eyes of every man present. The Lone Star jewels. A red diamond, a black opal and a two-carat emerald, represented an unspoken mantra—lifelong values they vowed to uphold.

With satisfied nods, Ben, Matt and Justin departed. They had agreed beforehand that Aaron and Dakota would wait for the construction crew.

The diplomat headed out to his truck and returned with a thermos and two plastic cups. He placed them on a nearby bench. "Shall we?"

"Sure," Dakota answered. "And I'm glad it was you and not Justin who supplied the coffee."

Aaron poured the steaming brew, and they grinned at each other in the dark. It was a running joke that the doctor had acquired a taste for week-old sludge that accumulated in the bottom of a pot.

"So how does it feel to be back on American soil?" Aaron asked.

"Good. It's where I belong, I suppose." Even if an edge of restlessness had begun to set in. For Dakota the end of an assignment often left him anxious.

The other man lifted his coffee. "If you get hungry, my wife sent along some pastries. They're in the truck."

"Thanks. Maybe later." Although Dakota considered Aaron a close friend, they went on to discuss insignificant things. Aaron wasn't one to pry, and Dakota wasn't one to offer details about his personal life. Aaron already knew that Kathy had left the Foreign Service and was staying with Dakota until she found a suitable place of her own. What else could be said of his broken marriage? Dakota had offered Kathy a guest room at the ranch so they could pursue friendship. He wasn't supposed to want her so badly, wasn't supposed to hurt every time he thought about the past. Admitting how he felt would solve nothing.

An hour after the sun came up, Aaron opened the gate for the construction crew, a trio of men who routinely repaired the hardscape at the park.

Dakota leaned against a tree as they poured the concrete. After the barricades were placed, he and Aaron would discuss another construction matter with the crew, but only for the sake of their cover. The American diplomat and the retired air force lieutenant would remain at the scene to protect the Lone Star jewels one last time.

A small breeze billowed Dakota's jacket. Within days the pool would be filled, and only those who had made a vow to the Texas Cattleman's Club would know that three priceless gems lay beneath the reflection of Tex Langley's statue.

Kathy knew she was alone. Dakota had left the ranch in the wee hours of the morning. The master bedroom was next to hers, and she'd heard his shower running at an ungodly hour.

Squinting at the sunlight streaming through the windows, she slipped on her robe, then stepped into the hall. Glancing over her shoulder, she noticed Dakota's door was slightly ajar.

She had no right to enter the master bedroom, but she couldn't seem to stop herself. Immediately the bed drew her toward it. She ran her hand along the wood and imagined Dakota sleeping there, his long muscular body tangled in the sheets. He was a light sleeper, a man who always seemed to have something on his mind.

The room looked the same. He'd kept it just the way she had decorated it. The horse weather vane still stood atop a Chippendale desk, the window valances still matched the fabric on the canopy bed and a hand-painted dresser displayed a collection of Indian baskets and crystal candelabras.

Kathy released a shaky breath. Still scanning the dresser, she noticed a familiar item was missing. A framed photograph. A picture of herself and Dakota on their wedding day. She moved closer and reached for the top drawer. Had he buried it beneath his clothes? Or had he destroyed it?

"What are you looking for?"

Caught in the act, Kathy froze, her fingers wrapped around the brass handle. "I apologize," she said as she turned toward him. "I shouldn't have come in here."

He stood, tall and rigid in black jeans, leather boots and a lightweight jacket. The brim of a cowboy hat shielded his eyes, but she knew they were fixed on her.

"I asked what you were looking for."

He made her feel like a criminal, the woman who had once shared this room with him, slept in the canopy bed, kept her undergarments folded in the drawer she had been opening. "I wondered where our picture was," she answered honestly.

He jutted his chin toward the dresser. "It's in there. I couldn't look at it. Not every day."

"I'm sorry," Kathy whispered, not knowing what else to say. His tone was guarded, but pain edged his words. She knew she owed him an explanation, yet she didn't know where to begin.

Neither spoke after that, and Kathy felt the room closing in. She glanced back at the dresser and imagined their picture hidden beneath his clothes. It made her sad and guilty. He deserved better than a woman who had just walked away, a woman who couldn't bring herself to admit why she had left. But the loss of their child and the loneliness she had suffered wasn't something she could put into words. It wasn't fair, but it made her realize that she and Dakota had never really been friends. Their courtship had been a whirlwind romance based on passion, not communication. And their marriage had been much the same.

Dakota followed her gaze to the dresser. "I don't burn candles anymore. I don't know why I still keep them around."

She understood his meaning. Their wedding picture used to sit between the crystal candelabras, and they used to make love by candlelight, touch and kiss while blue and gold flames sent shadows flickering across their skin.

"I'm sorry," she said again. Sorry that she had hurt him. Sorry they hadn't been able to share more than just their bodies. But she knew he hid his deepest emotions. She had seen him laugh, but she had never seen him cry. Not even at his father's funeral.

He tossed his hat onto the bed. "I'm sorry, too. I didn't

mean to sound so harsh earlier. I just didn't expect to come home and find you in my room."

She wasn't sure whether to leave him alone or stay and talk. He still seemed guarded, yet his tone had softened, his apology sincere. "You left while it was still dark."

"Texas Cattleman's Club meeting." He unzipped his jacket, then dragged a hand through his hair. "We secured the jewels."

And he seemed unsettled, she thought, a little edgy. But hiding the jewels meant the mission was truly over and he had become an out-of-work soldier again, a man without a purpose. Staying home never suited Dakota, and that was one of the reasons Kathy had left. She had wanted some normalcy in their marriage, but he had been satisfied with their whirl-wind relationship, with stealing moments between his never-ending missions.

"Are you sure it's okay for me to stay here?" she asked, wondering if it had been a mistake.

"Of course, it's okay."

He came toward her, so close she could smell the wind on his clothes, the fading scent of his aftershave. She lifted her face to his and wondered if he was going to kiss her. If he did, she would kiss him back. She could feel the sexual mag-net, the energy that drew them together. They couldn't talk, but they could touch. Yearn for each other.

He toyed with the collar of her chenille robe. "What hap-pened to the silky one?"

"I didn't think I should wear it around you."

He moistened his lips. "Afraid I wouldn't be able to con-trol myself?"

She swallowed. "It's been known to happen." He was too tall, too dark, too dangerously handsome. His mouth was inches from hers, his breath warm. He would taste like the elements, she decided, like a warrior who belonged to the night.

He skimmed her cheek with his, then stepped back and grinned. "So you decided to wear this grandma getup in-stead?"

For a moment Kathy only stared. He'd gone from brooding to sexy to silly within the blink of an eye. And she remained in a daze, waiting for him to kiss her. She lifted her hand to her face, to the spot he'd just touched. "Grandma getup?"

"Yep. You look cute, though. Kinda sweet and fuzzy."

She couldn't find it within herself to return his smile. He teased her, but the humor hadn't quite reached his eyes. They were black, with a sort of feverish glow. He was aroused and pretending he wasn't. If she bumped against his fly, she'd feel the evidence of his desire. This was her punishment for invading his room, she thought. She should have stayed away.

He stepped back even farther. "Kathy?"

"Yes?"

"I danced with other women at the Texas Cattleman's Club ball. It was months ago, but I just thought I should mention it. You know I'm not one for fancy social events, but I felt more or less obligated to be there."

"And you felt obligated to dance." She tried to keep her voice steady. She had no right to be jealous. She had, after all, walked out on him. "It doesn't matter, Dakota. You didn't do anything wrong."

"Have you danced with other men?"

She sent him a twisted smile. "I danced with Payune. Remember?"

He didn't seem amused. "That's not what I mean."

"There were political functions in Washington. I suppose I danced a few times." But she couldn't remember who her partners were. "I don't understand why you brought this up."

"Because you've lived alone for three years. And I keep thinking that there must have been men interested in you. Someone must have asked you on a date."

The look in his eyes startled her. The macho, possessive glare. She had already told him that she hadn't slept with anyone, but apparently he couldn't stand the image of her even having dinner with another man. "I didn't go on any dates."

His gaze softened. "So what did you do?"

"Worked." Came home to an empty apartment and

thought about her husband, wondered what he was doing, wondered if his next assignment would be a greater risk than the last, if he would be captured or killed. "I adopted a dog."

"Really? That's great."

"I'm glad you think so because I'm picking Sugar up at the airport tomorrow. A friend from Washington is putting her on a plane for me."

"Sugar? That's your dog's name?"

Kathy nodded. "She belonged to an elderly lady who lived in my building. And when Mrs. Leone died, I just sort of inherited her dog. But Sugar is a little angel. I adore her." The Maltese had gotten her through some sad and lonely times, making her separation from Dakota bearable. "She loves everyone. And she's quiet. You won't even know she's around."

"Your dog is welcome here, Kathy. You have to stop acting like you're putting me out. I invited you, remember? We agreed to be friends."

"Yes, friends," she said, wondering if that was truly possible.

The following day Kathy returned from the airport with the Maltese in tow. She walked into the living room, and Dakota looked up from his newspaper and smiled.

The dog was pretty much what he had expected. Little old ladies had lapdogs that wore bows on top of their heads, and Kathy had inherited Sugar from a little old lady. He had to admit the pooch was cute—silky white fur and a face with round eyes and a delicate muzzle. He figured the Maltese didn't weigh any more than four or five pounds.

Placing the paper on the coffee table, he came to his feet. "So this is Sugar?" He reached out to pet the dog and received a high-pitched doggie yip in return.

Kathy's head whipped up. "What happened?"

"I don't know." Dakota nearly stammered. "I guess she's scared or something."

"But she likes people." Kathy adjusted Sugar in her arms. "She never acts that way."

"She just got off a plane, and this is a new environment. Hell, she's bound to be nervous."

"I suppose you're right." Kathy stroked the dog's head. "Maybe I should put her down and let her get used to the place."

Sugar decided she liked the couch. She curled up on a cowhide pillow, and Dakota thought she looked like a toy— a little, white fluffball on his rugged sofa. Yep, she was cute, even if he thought hair bows on canines were kind of sissy. But this one was a female, so he supposed that was okay.

He inched closer, then knelt to let the dog sniff his hand.

Sugar bared her teeth and snarled.

Caught completely off guard, Dakota jerked back, lost his balance and landed flat on his startled butt.

Behind him, Kathy gasped. "Oh, my God! Are you all right?"

"Of course, I am."

"Did she bite you?"

"No." With as much masculine pride as he could muster, he stood and squared his shoulders. He outweighed Sugar by a good hundred and eighty pounds. And he was an ex-military man trained in survival tactics. A former para rescuer who flew planes into enemy territory, rescued hostages, defused mines, tracked gunrunners across the desert. He had done it all, in and out of the service.

"I wasn't expecting her to snarl at me," he said, explaining away the humiliation.

"I'm so sorry. She's never done that to anyone before." Kathy reprimanded Sugar, and the dog dropped her ears and whined, making Dakota feel like a heel.

"I'm sure it won't happen again," she told him.

"Don't worry about it." He met Kathy's gaze, and she caught her bottom lip between her teeth. "Don't you dare laugh," he warned.

"Why would I?" she asked, a bit too innocently.

"Oh, I don't know. Maybe because your little dog knocked me on my ass."

"You should have seen yourself, Dakota."

Her lip quivered, and they both burst into laughter. But when footsteps sounded in the entryway, Kathy sobered immediately.

"That must be Mrs. Miller," she said.

Dakota nodded. He knew Kathy and the housekeeper hadn't seen each other yet, but he figured they were about to. Mrs. Miller would say a predictable yet impersonal hello before she began her chores.

Dakota studied his wife. As though suddenly conscious of her appearance, she fussed with the loose strands of her hair—that luscious, heavy hair she had twisted into its usual chignon. This afternoon she sported tan trousers and a lemon-colored blouse. Yellow suited her. Even the sunny robe she'd worn yesterday had turned him on. She'd looked as frothy as the meringue on top of a pie.

Mrs. Miller entered the room like a broom-wielding militant, shoulders back, head held high, short gray hair resembling a helmet. She could have been a nurse with her crisp white uniform and thick-soled shoes. It amazed Dakota that even after a thorough housecleaning, she departed as starched and white as she had arrived.

"Good afternoon, Lieutenant," she said, greeting him as she had for the past ten years.

"Good afternoon," he responded as the older lady turned toward Kathy.

He watched as they acknowledged each other. Kathy stepped forward and smiled. "It's nice to see you again."

"Thank you. It's a pleasure to see you as well."

The conversation was neither strained nor friendly. Dakota had no idea if Mrs. Miller liked Kathy, but he wasn't sure if the older woman liked him, either. The housekeeper rarely smiled, even during the holidays when she filled the cookie jar with red-nosed reindeers and jolly Santas.

Mrs. Miller smoothed her immaculate dress, then turned and spotted the dog curled up on the couch. "Oh, my."

"That's Sugar," Kathy said. "But she's a little nervous today."

As the older lady headed toward the sofa, Dakota searched

for a more appropriate warning. Be careful. Watch yourself. That adorable little fluffball is actually a junkyard Doberman in disguise. But before he could utter a single word, Sugar wiggled her behind and gazed up at Mrs. Miller with adoring eyes.

"Aren't you precious?" the housekeeper crooned in a singsong voice Dakota had never heard the no-nonsense woman use before.

Kathy beamed like a moon in June, and within minutes she and Mrs. Miller were discussing Sugar's upkeep and habits. The dog ate a select brand of canned food, played indoor fetch games, required periodic trips to a groomer and enjoyed being walked on a silver leash that matched her glittery collar.

Dakota had never felt so left out, so big and undeniably male. And then it hit him. *Male.* That was it. Sugar probably didn't know what to make of him. She wasn't used to men. The Maltese had been coddled and protected by women.

He watched the pooch leap into Kathy's arms, watched as Kathy's expression turned soft and gentle.

Dakota swallowed around a lump in his throat. Somehow he was going to have to earn that little dog's trust. At the moment Sugar seemed to hold the key to Kathy's heart—a heart he longed to feel beating in time with his own. Because in spite of all of his friendship talk, Dakota couldn't deny the truth.

He was still in love with his wife.

Seven

Later that afternoon Dakota offered to accompany Kathy on her home search. Royal had plenty of upscale apartment buildings since it was a bustling, exclusively rich town surrounded by oil fields and sprawling ranches.

The temperature rose to ninety degrees, but the West Texas wind blew, making the heat bearable. Kathy still wore the lemon-colored blouse, and her hair still rebelled from the pins struggling to secure it. Wispy tendrils fluttered around her face, reflecting sunlight like sparks of fire.

They took the stairs and followed the apartment manager to 6B, then waited while the woman unlocked the door. Kathy had specific tastes, but she hadn't been nearly as selective as Dakota. He had found fault with the previous apartments they'd looked at, but he had good reason. Plain and simple— he didn't want his wife leaving the ranch. He liked having her around. He wanted to keep her.

He loved her.

"This is nice," Kathy said as they entered.

Dakota frowned. "It's all right."

A gas fireplace dominated the living room and two large windows offered a spectacular view of Royal. The appliances in the spacious kitchen were new, and the dining area boasted a brass chandelier.

"That won't look right with your furniture," Dakota said. "It's too modern for antiques."

"It's fine," Kathy responded and moved on to explore the bedrooms.

The master suite presented another view, this one from a rather large balcony. Dakota couldn't find much fault, but he was damned determined to try. "I'll bet lugging groceries up and down stairs is a nuisance. And then of course there's that balcony."

Kathy stepped onto the feature in question. "What's wrong with it?"

He moved to stand next to her, out of earshot from the building manager. "Could be dangerous."

She sent him a strange look. "It seems sturdy enough to me."

"Of course, it's sturdy. I was referring to the rail. Sugar might be able to fit through the bars." He approached the rail, playing out his drama. "It's a long way down, sweetheart. And there's nothing to pad the fall. I don't think you should risk it."

Kathy studied the opening between the bars with a critical eye. "Sugar's body is bigger than that. She couldn't fit through there."

Dakota scraped a booted foot on the cement. He was certain Kathy would have given that scenario more thought. "Maybe you're right. But she could get her head stuck. Animals do that sort of thing all the time."

That appeared to do the trick. Kathy frowned and stepped closer to the rail. "You know, that's actually possible."

"Of course it is." He resisted the urge to flash an overly smug, overly macho smile. "Did you think I was making these things up? I've been trained to spot potential hazards.

And this apartment isn't right for you. I sensed it the moment we walked in.''

She gave him another one of those strange looks, and he lost the urge to grin, his machismo not quite so smug. Had he really said something that ridiculous, laid it on that thick? Trained to spot potential hazards? In an upscale Royal apartment?

"How about some lunch?" he suggested, hoping to distract her. Did he really want her to know that he was deliberately thwarting her effort to find a suitable place to live?

Kathy accepted his invitation, so Dakota decided on the Royal Diner, a typical greasy-spoon-type place that served typical greasy-spoon-type food. He had a hankering for casual atmosphere and a messy hamburger. He'd been to enough fancy balls and eaten enough deviled quail eggs to last a lifetime.

They scooted into a vinyl booth and grinned at each other like kids sharing a private joke. The paper placemat the waitress slapped in front of them boasted, The Royal Diner—Food Fit for a King! Yet King Bertram stopping in for a bowl of chili and finding it to his liking presented a ludicrous image.

Dakota ordered a bacon cheeseburger, and Kathy chose a club sandwich. He drank coffee while she sipped iced tea.

"I really thought I would find an apartment today," she said.

"You know what the problem is?" he asked without giving her a chance to answer. "You should be living in a house and not an apartment. Someplace with a yard for Sugar and privacy for yourself." Someplace like the ranch, he thought. He had a fenced yard the pooch could play in and a big canopy bed just waiting for Kathy.

"You know, I think you're right," she responded, her eyes sparkling with sudden enthusiasm. "I should start looking at rental houses instead."

Dakota wondered if he was an idiot. Here he was hoping to keep her, yet he hadn't asked why she'd left in the first place. Lifting his coffee to hide a frown, he took a sip. And why hadn't he asked?

Because deep down he feared the answer. Kathy might have left for a very simple, very devastating reason. She might have fallen out of love with him. And if that was the case, there wasn't much he could do about it.

Or was there? If she had loved him once, couldn't she love him again? If they spent enough time together, would those feelings come back?

The waitress delivered their lunch, and as they sampled their food, the jukebox played a country ballad. The sound of silverware clanking and voices chattering could be heard above the music, but the song managed to soothe Dakota's soul just the same. Kathy had chosen to live in Royal. That in itself seemed like a good sign.

He searched her gaze. "Do you ever think about the first time we met?"

A small smile touched her lips. "Charity dinner at the Texas Cattleman's Club. You were in uniform."

"And you were in white silk." A dress as cool and sleek as the woman wearing it. He'd taken one long, luxurious look and decided he'd wanted her. As to how he intended to win her over, he hadn't been sure. "I didn't think you would be interested. You were so refined, so elegant. Your type rarely gave me the time of day."

"My type?"

"You know what I mean." He took another bite of his burger and swallowed. "Do you think it was fate, us meeting like we did?" He had been stationed at Aviano Air Base in northeastern Italy at the time, but was home on leave. And she had come to Royal to visit Aaron before she left for Italy to replace a consular who had taken ill.

"That we met in Royal, but both ended up at the same Italian village?" She glanced down at her sandwich, then back up. "The Italy part might have been fate, but Aaron suspected I wanted to meet you. I think that's why he invited me to the charity dinner."

Stunned, Dakota leaned against the table. "I don't understand. Did Aaron mention me? Tell you I was a decent guy or something?"

Kathy stirred her tea a little nervously. "Yes, but I saw your picture first. Aaron had some photographs from a friend's wedding, and you were the best man. So when I came across your picture, I think I said something like 'Wow. He's gorgeous. Who is he?'" She clanked her spoon against the glass. "Pretty shallow, I guess."

Shallow? It was the best damn thing he'd heard in years. "Why didn't you ever tell me this before?"

"In the beginning it would have been too embarrassing. And later on, it didn't seem important. We never talked about how we had met."

Something in her voice bothered him. Something that said they weren't as close as he liked to remember. Dakota reached for his coffee, pushing his worry aside. Why dwell on the past? Instead he would do his best to focus on the future.

The following afternoon Kathy paced her bedroom, wondering what to do with herself. She couldn't seem to concentrate on anything other than overwhelming guilt. She could barely face herself in the mirror, let alone face Dakota every day.

Was he waiting for her to approach him? Waiting to hear why she had walked away from their marriage? A week had passed since they'd returned from Asterland, but she had yet to say a word.

It wasn't fair. He had a right to know. The baby had belonged to him, too.

Kathy slipped on a denim blouse, then zipped her jeans. She knew Dakota was at the barn, spending some time with the horses.

Exiting the house through the back door, she ventured into the Texas air. She could have taken one of Dakota's trucks, but decided the walk would do her good. Once inside the courtyard, she stopped to take comfort in her surroundings. Greenery had a way of soothing her, and the yard was lush with potted blooms. Beyond the Spanish tiles and rustic patio furniture lay a thick carpet of grass. This was her favorite spot at the ranch, a place to sip coffee in the morning and watch the stars light up the sky at night.

She opened the gate leading to the rest of the property. The land was flat, wide open and picturesque in a vast, Texas kind of way. As she walked, her boots kicked up dust. The soil wasn't fertile, but it reflected the sun in warm, golden shades.

The breezeway barn stood strong and solid, a building alive with the scents and sounds of the horses Dakota loved. He had an incredible facility, designed with the recreational cowboy in mind—an indoor and outdoor arena, fenced pastures, wash racks, a hot walker, an enormous tack room, hay storage and RV buildings. He didn't want for anything, she thought, except maybe the truth from his wife.

Kathy didn't need to enter the barn. Dakota stood beside a hitching post, saddling a big, black gelding. She couldn't help but admire her husband, the breadth of his shoulders, taper of his waist, those long legs covered in time-worn denim. And his rear, she thought, that taut masculine rear.

She walked toward him, and he turned and smiled, making her guilty heart flutter. He still affected her, still had a way of making her limbs watery and her breath catch.

"Hi," she said. "Are you going for a ride?" It was a dumb question with an obvious answer, but she couldn't think of anything else to say.

"Sure am. Do you want to join me? It's a great day to hit the trail. Not nearly as hot as yesterday."

Kathy brushed a stray hair from her eye. He sounded so relaxed, so friendly. And she was a nervous wreck, at least on the inside. Maybe on the outside, too. She couldn't seem to keep her hands still. She batted away another hair, a useless effort in the wind.

"Okay," she answered, thinking she would probably return to the ranch wobbly-legged and sore. "But I haven't been on a horse in a while. I'm a little out of practice." And anxiety-ridden. Could she really talk about the miscarriage today? Talk about their lost baby on this warm, breezy Texas day?

"Then you should ride Serenity," he said, suggesting Kathy's favorite mount. "She'll be good to you."

Serenity had been named well. The mare, a leopard Appaloosa, nuzzled Kathy in a gentle welcome. "She hasn't forgotten me."

Dakota placed Kathy's saddle on a nearby stand. "You're not easy to forget, sweetheart."

And neither was he, she thought, sending him a shaky smile. Not a day had passed without him entering her mind.

They mounted their horses in silence. The main trail led to a dozen smaller paths, the next as boundless as the last. The vegetation was sparse and the ground level for as far as the eye could see, but the land was rich with history. Wars, cattle drives, the building of railroads, the discovery of oil. Every rock, every cactus, every speck of dirt told a story.

They rode for nearly two hours, with Kathy taking in familiar sights, scenery she enjoyed. In the distance, windmills turned, pumping water from the earth.

"Do you want to stop?" Dakota asked as they came upon one of the few shade trees on the trail.

Kathy nodded, anxiety setting in once again. If she intended to tell him, then it should be now, while they were away from the ranch—away from the memories that lingered in the halls of the house they once shared.

She slid from her saddle, and Dakota took Serenity's reins. He hobbled the horses, returning with a blanket under his arm. Dakota never traveled on horseback without a blanket. It was, Kathy decided, the Indian in him, the nomad running through his veins. The Comanche were a wandering tribe, a people who had once roamed West Texas, then later fought to keep the Lone Star plains as their home. Another piece of history, she thought, another lost battle.

They sat beneath the oak and sipped bottled water.

"I'm going out of town tonight," he said.

Kathy's heart made a fast, nervous leap. "Another assignment already?"

He shook his head. "No. Business in Lubbock."

"Oh." She released an audible breath. Business in Lubbock meant the shopping centers Dakota owned. Commercial property was the major source of his income. The Texas Cattleman's Club missions had nothing to do with money. "How long will you be gone?"

"A few days."

Apparently that was all the information he intended to share. But Kathy knew Dakota didn't enjoy the corporate world. It wasn't dangerous enough, she supposed.

He removed his Stetson and handed it to her. "You'd better wear my hat on the way back or you'll end up with a sunburn."

"Thanks." Kathy placed the hat beside her. She had the fair, sensitive skin common to most natural redheads, even though she lacked the freckles and fiery temper often associated with scarlet hair. But Dakota used to say that her passion was red, that her appetite in bed was the color of fire.

She felt her cheeks warm. "I'm probably pink already."

"A little." He tapped her nose in an affectionate gesture, and her nipples pebbled.

"This is nice," he said.

She blinked. "Nice?"

"The weather. The horses. You and me. It reminds me of our days in Italy."

It had been wondrous—falling in love with a pilot, holding his hand and stealing kisses in tiny cafés. Aviano Air Base was thirty minutes from the beach and thirty minutes from the mountains. A more romantic location didn't exist.

He reclined on the blanket. "Lie down with me."

Kathy caught her breath. She couldn't resist—not his crooked smile, his Texas drawl, the long fluid line of his body.

She lowered herself to the blanket. Being next to him was more than nice.

"I think we're turning out to be pretty good friends," he said. "Don't you?"

She nodded, knowing she couldn't bear to spoil this moment, this warm, tender feeling. She couldn't tell him why she had left. At least not today.

* * *

Kathy answered the phone at 10:00 p.m., surprised by the masculine voice on the other end of the line. Dakota rarely called when he was away on business.

"What are you doing?" he asked.

"Nothing, really." She glanced at her bed. Sugar was curled up on a pillow. "I was thinking I might make some hot chocolate. Maybe read for a while."

"Are you in the kitchen?"

"No. My room."

"And you're alone?"

Kathy gripped the phone. "Sugar's here."

Dakota sounded strange, not quite himself. She looked around nervously. Was he worried the house was bugged? He could be involved in another mission, something he hadn't told her about. Or someone from his past might have surfaced. Dakota had probably made plenty of enemies over the years.

"Are you on the cordless phone?" he asked.

Was he really in Lubbock? "Yes."

"Good. I want you to go to my room."

"Okay." Heart pounding, she walked down the hall, then entered the master bedroom. He hadn't made the bed before he'd left, but other than that, the room was tidy. Nothing looked disturbed, nothing out of place. "I'm here."

Dakota's voice softened. "Go to the closet and pick out one of my shirts."

Kathy frowned. His instructions were getting stranger by the minute, but he appeared to have a distinct purpose in mind, something he needed her to do. Meet him somewhere? Bring him a shirt? It made no sense.

She stepped into the walk-in closet. Neat, organized, very Dakota. Casual wear at one end, dress clothes at the other. She tried to ignore the empty rack that used to be hers. He hadn't filled the space. It remained vacant.

"What kind of shirt?" she asked.

"It doesn't matter. You choose."

She reached for denim, soft and well-worn—a long-sleeved

shirt with pearl-front snaps. She liked how he looked in blue, it made his eyes appear darker, his skin more golden.

"Do you have one?"

"Yes."

"Put it on the bed."

If they were being bugged, she thought, someone was listening to an odd conversation. But maybe that was the idea. She removed the shirt from the hanger and did as he asked. "Done."

"Good girl. Now tell me what you're wearing."

Kathy froze. She looked around, caught sight of the canopy bed—the tousled covers, his denim shirt. There were no electronic bugs, no old enemies lurking. She wasn't in any danger. And there was only one reason why she couldn't hang up on him.

His voice. The husky, sensual sound of his voice.

She adjusted the phone. "I can't believe you're doing this to me."

"I'm lonely, Kathy. I miss you."

She closed her eyes. She missed him, too.

"Are you wearing a dress?" he asked.

She shook her head, then realized he couldn't see her. "No." He wanted to see her, she thought. He wanted to picture her in his mind. She opened her eyes. "A blouse and a skirt."

"Nylons?"

"No. My legs are bare."

She heard him swallow. "Take your blouse off."

Kathy sat on the edge of the bed. Could she do this? Could she play this forbidden game? She touched his shirt. Dakota's scent lingered in the room, the woodsy note of his cologne drifting through the air.

"Kathy?"

"I'm taking it off," she said, reaching for the top button on her blouse.

"Is it green? Emerald, like your eyes?"

"Yes." But even if it wasn't, she would have told him what he wanted to hear. She wanted to fuel his imagination, make him warm and aroused. She glanced at her hand and realized she still wore her wedding ring. "Where are you, Dakota?"

"In a hotel room."

She pictured him lying on a bed, his chest bare, his back braced against a wooden headboard. His room-service dinner would be untouched, except for a bottle of imported beer. She could almost taste the alcohol on his lips, taste the intoxicating flavor.

"Are you wearing jeans?"

"Yes."

She let the blouse fall from her shoulders. "Are they unzipped?"

His voice turned rough. "As far down as they'll go."

Suddenly the image in her mind intensified. The contrast of his skin against crisp, white sheets. The broad expanse of his chest, the narrow line of his hips. His sex, full and erect, pressing against his jeans.

Kathy couldn't stop the heat between her legs, the silky moisture. "I'm in my bra and panties." She had dropped her skirt to the floor, where it pooled at her feet.

Dakota groaned, and she knew he had lifted his hips. "Tell me what you look like," he said. "Every detail."

She walked to the mirror, the phone cradled against her ear. She looked aroused, her cheeks flushed, her lips slightly parted. "My hair is pinned up, but it's starting to fall." Just the way he liked it, she thought, tangled and messy. And the color of her bra, she told him, was called autumn gold. She had ordered it from a catalog, along with matching panties. The bra was seamless and sheer, the panties decorated with a hint of lace.

"I can hear the wind," she said, turning toward the window. She could almost feel it blowing through her hair, cooling her face. With her head tipped back and her eyes closed, she unhooked her bra, then slipped off her panties.

"Are you naked?" he asked, his voice a husky whisper above the wind.

"Yes." For him, she thought. Naked for him.

"Put my shirt on, Kathy. Put it on and climb under the covers. I want you in my bed."

The shirt could have been his hands. It caressed her, brushed her nipples, slid between her thighs—rough yet gentle.

And the bed. She pressed her face to the pillow and imagined him there. His scent. The weight of his erection. His mouth covering hers.

Kathy brought the phone to her lips and smiled. Tonight they would make love in their minds. Warm, wet, languorous love. A beautiful, erotic fantasy.

Kathy answered the door, and found herself face-to-face with Violet Tenewa, Dakota's Comanche mother.

"Kathy!" the other woman exclaimed. "Honey, I had no idea you were back."

"I'm not. I mean, I am, but…" How could she explain her presence at the ranch to her mother-in-law? "I'm just a temporary houseguest. Dakota invited me to stay until I find another place to live."

Violet's smile fell. "Oh."

Kathy stepped away from the door, praying this wasn't going to be an awkward reunion. She adored Dakota's mother. Violet was a striking, independent woman. Even at sixty-two, she looked as exotic as her name. Her silver-streaked hair fell in a straight, black curtain, complementing a golden complexion and deep-set eyes.

"Would you like to come in?" Kathy asked. "Dakota isn't here, but I'd love to visit with you."

"Thank you. I'd love to visit with you, too."

Kathy made a pot of coffee and warmed the pastries she had baked the day before. Coffee in hand, they sat in the living room, the aroma of cinnamon wafting between them.

"Where is Dakota?" Violet asked.

"He had some business in Lubbock. He's been gone a few days."

Violet reached for a cinnamon roll. "Have you heard from him?"

"Yes, he called." And seduced me over the phone, she thought, her skin suddenly warm. "He should be home later this afternoon."

Neither spoke after that. Small talk didn't seem appropriate. Kathy had walked out on Violet's son—a subject that certainly outweighed the weather.

"I'm sorry," Kathy said finally, struggling to find a simple way to explain the burden in her heart. "I never meant to hurt Dakota. When I left, I kept hoping that he would come to me. That he—" She paused, her eyes beginning to mist. "That he would tell me that I was more important than his work." She swallowed past the emotion and met the other woman's gaze. "I suppose that sounds foolish, especially to someone as independent as you. Your life with Jack was so unconventional."

"Oh, honey. It doesn't sound foolish at all."

Kathy scooted to the edge of the sofa. "Then you understand why I left?"

Violet pursed her lips. "I suppose I do. Except it's a little difficult for me to accept because he's my son. I want to believe that Dakota was a perfect husband, even if he wasn't."

Kathy's eyes turned misty again. "I never stopped loving him."

Violet squeezed her hand. "Now that part I truly understand. I know it's possible to love a man who always has other priorities. Who makes you feel like you're second-best in his heart."

Unable to conceal her curiosity, Kathy blinked away her tears. "Dakota's father?"

Violet nodded. "If Jack Lewis wasn't caught up in an important business deal, then he was attending a social function with his wife." She released a heavy sigh and went on, "I realize that I shouldn't have been involved with a married man, but I honestly believed he was going to divorce his wife and marry me. Jack and Sharon had one of those society marriages. There wasn't any real love between them."

"We've never talked about this before." Kathy knew Violet had been Jack's mistress, but she had no idea Dakota's mother had wanted something more. "I assumed you were comfortable with the arrangement."

"No, I never was."

"But you were with him all those years."

"Yes, all those years, and he was still married to Sharon. They even died together."

A boating accident, Kathy recalled. "I'm sorry. I had no idea." Which seemed disrespectful to Dakota's mother. Most women would prefer to be a wife than a mistress.

"I was nineteen when I met Jack. Nineteen and naive. I left him once, though. I was devastated that I was about to give birth, and my baby's father still hadn't made arrangements to marry me. So I went to South Dakota to stay with a friend." She sent Kathy a woman-to-woman smile. "Two months later I came back to Texas."

Kathy returned Violet's smile. "And presented Jack with a son."

"An illegitimate son. Something Dakota never let himself forget."

Both of their smiles faded. "But he hasn't made an issue of it, at least not to me. I was under the impression it didn't matter to him all that much."

"It mattered." Violet reached for her coffee, then took a sip. "Being the illegitimate son of a prominent man wasn't easy, even if Jack treated him well. Dakota tried very hard to legitimize himself, to be accepted by his father's peers. And I suppose serving his country was a way of proving his worth. Dakota enlisted at seventeen, a boy on the verge of manhood."

And now Kathy understood why her husband didn't enjoy high-society events. They reminded him of a time when he wasn't welcome. "It must have made things easier on Dakota that Jack and Sharon didn't have any children. At least he was Jack's only son."

"That's true, but his father being intimate with two women

was still a problem. I don't think Dakota understands the true concept of marriage—how much work is involved or how much a couple has to give of themselves. In that respect, Jack was a poor role model.''

Kathy nodded. It made sense. All of it. Unlike his father, Dakota had remained faithful to his vows, but he still didn't consider marriage the number-one priority in his life. His career had always come first.

"Dakota still doesn't know why I left. I can't seem to bring myself to say the words out loud. At least not to him.'' And that sounded like an excuse, Kathy thought. Feeble and unfair. But there was the baby she had wanted so badly—the part of her heart she had lost.

Violet frowned. "Has he asked? Has he questioned you about it at all?''

"No.''

"Then maybe he isn't ready to face the past. Maybe he needs a little more time to sort out his feelings.''

Kathy cocked her head, considering the possibility. "I hadn't thought of that.'' She hadn't thought of anything but her guilt, her secret, her own loss. But what Violet suggested provided a small measure of relief. Kathy wasn't ready to talk about the past, and Dakota wasn't ready to hear about it. "After I left, did he confide in you? Did he say anything?''

"Not a word,'' the other woman responded in a soft, almost sad voice. "At first he closed himself off completely, and later he threw himself into his work, doing all of those dangerous things that he does.''

Kathy lifted her coffee. Dangerous things. She understood that phrase well. "So he—'' As a pair of boots sounded on the Spanish tile, she nearly spilled the hot drink.

Dakota.

"He's home.'' She looked up at Violet, and they both waited for him to enter the room.

Eight

While Kathy battled a bout of nervousness, Violet stood and approached her son. Had he overheard their conversation? Kathy wondered.

She stole a quick glance and decided he hadn't. It wasn't in Dakota's nature to eavesdrop.

"Mom." He hugged her, then stepped back. "It's good to see you."

"Kathy said you were in Lubbock."

He nodded. "I had some business to take care of with Dad's properties."

Kathy shifted on the couch. Strange, she thought, how Dakota still hadn't taken mental possession of the shopping centers Jack had left him. He still referred to them as his father's—a man who had influenced him more than she had realized.

Violet resumed her seat, and Dakota turned toward Kathy. "Hi."

"Hi." She met his gaze, her heart leaping into its teeter-totter mode. Why couldn't she look at him without experiencing a physical reaction? "I wasn't expecting you back so soon."

"I had a meeting this morning, but it ended early."

He held her gaze, and her heart continued to flutter. He wore a tan T-shirt, faded blue jeans and distressed leather boots—clothes too casual for a business meeting. Apparently he had changed before coming home.

Kathy chewed her lip. Were those the Wranglers he had worn during their telephone conversation? Unable to help herself, she glanced at his fly, then back up to his face. He flashed a bedroom smile and made her hot all over.

Are you wearing jeans?

Yes.

Are they unzipped?

As far down as they'll go.

Violet cleared her throat, and Kathy felt like a teenager who'd been caught lusting after an older boy. Her nipples tingled against her bra, not a good thing to happen when the older boy's observant mother occupied the same room.

Dakota looked away and pulled a hand through his hair. "So, Mom, what's going on? What made you stop by?"

"Do I need a special reason to come to your house?"

"No, of course not."

Violet's eyes, Kathy noticed, sparkled with amusement. But her big, strong, Comanche son revealed something rare—an embarrassed flush coloring his bronzed cheeks. Of course, he had been caught behaving like a teenager, too—sending Kathy a provocative, I'm-thinking-about-sex smile.

Dakota moved toward a leather recliner and sat. Careful, it seemed, not to cast his gaze in Kathy's direction. He focused on his mother instead.

Unwelcome silence ensued, and Kathy wished her heart would quit bumping against her breast. Violet couldn't possibly know that she had climbed into Dakota's bed while he was gone, or that his shirt had brushed decadently between her naked thighs.

Two or three minutes passed, but still no one spoke. They

just sat there, Kathy and Dakota avoiding eye contact, and Violet splitting her amused gaze between them.

"Actually I did stop by for a reason," she admitted finally.

Grateful for the reprieve, Kathy's breath rushed out of her lungs. Dakota, too, seemed grateful his mother had decided to let them off the hook. He leaned forward in his chair.

"As you know," Violet said, "I'm on the board of directors at the West Texas Indian Center, and we need some volunteers to help out with an event next Saturday."

"What kind of an event?" Dakota asked.

"A carnival to raise money for the Foster Care Mentor Program."

Apparently more relaxed, Dakota strode to the bar and poured himself a soda water. "Oh, yeah. You mentioned that program before."

Violet explained to Kathy. "Since we're not able to place all of the children in Indian homes, we're trying to secure weekend foster parents. It's actually called respite care, but we prefer to think of it as our Mentor Program."

"That sounds wonderful," Kathy responded. "Role models are important." Especially to kids from troubled homes, she thought sadly.

"So you'll help out at the carnival?" the other woman asked.

"I'd love to."

Violet looked at Dakota, and he placed his drink on the bar. "Sure, Mom. Me, too."

"Good." She smiled at both of them. "I should get going. I still have more volunteers to recruit." She hugged Kathy, then took her son's arm as he walked her to the door.

Kathy busied herself carrying coffee cups and the leftover pastries into the kitchen. A minute later, Dakota came in and grabbed one of the sweets.

"I enjoyed visiting with your mom," she said before the lone moment trapped them into another awkward spell.

"I imagine she was surprised to see you. I should have called her and told her you were staying here."

"That's okay." Kathy didn't want to think about telephone

conversations, not when she couldn't get the other night out of her mind.

She rinsed the cups and placed them in the dishwasher, then turned to see Dakota licking icing from a cinnamon roll.

He smiled that sexy smile, and she swallowed.

"Do you want a bite?" he asked.

She wanted to bite him. Kiss and nibble. Taste that warm, dark, tantalizing skin.

Struggling to respond in a dignified voice, she cleared her throat and then remembered why Dakota's mother had done that earlier. "No, thank you," she managed.

Sugar trotted into the kitchen and saved Kathy's sanity. The dog made a wide circle around Dakota to get to her.

"She still doesn't like me," he said.

Kathy opened a can of dog food, glad the Maltese had given her another busy task. "I know, I'm sorry. I just don't understand it."

"I do." He leaned against the counter, his shoulder nearly brushing hers. "Sugar isn't used to men."

And he was definitely a man, she thought, cursing her quavering heart. Dakota Lewis was as rugged as his gender came.

She filled the dog's bowl, hardly blaming Sugar for being nervous around him. "Then I suppose it will take time."

Time she wouldn't allow herself to have. Soon she would have to find another place to live.

Dakota knew he didn't have much time. Several days had passed since he'd returned from Lubbock, and he'd barely seen Kathy. She spent every free moment looking at rentals. How was he supposed to win his wife back once she moved out?

Call her? Make love on the phone?

The idea had merit, but it wasn't the same as a flesh-to-flesh encounter. He missed holding her, missed being her husband.

And his progress with Sugar was slow, too. He opened the box of dog treats he kept in his room and stuffed a few in his pocket. He bribed the Maltese whenever Kathy wasn't around, although it didn't appear to do him much good. The dog still wouldn't get close enough to take the treat from his hand. He would set it on the floor, and she would wait until he backed away before nabbing it.

He strode down the hall, then entered the kitchen where he found Sugar with Mrs. Miller. The dog danced happily around the older woman's feet as she cleaned.

He assessed the situation. Little white dog. Big, dark Comanche man. Unless he got some outside help, his chances were slim to none with that pooch.

"Good morning, Mrs. Miller."

She looked up from her sponge. "Hello, Lieutenant."

He stood at attention, but why, he couldn't be sure. Mrs. Miller was hardly his superior. "I need a favor from you."

She took a break from her chore. "Yes, sir. What is it?"

"I want you to help me make friends with the dog." He eyed Sugar and noticed her ears had perked. "I'm not having much luck on my own."

Mrs. Miller cocked her head, giving him the same curious look as the dog. "What seems to be the trouble, Lieutenant?"

Dakota didn't ease his stance. At the moment he felt far from casual. What he felt, he realized, was tense. Out of his element. "Sugar doesn't appear to like men."

"Oh, my. That could present a problem."

She glanced at the dog, then back at Dakota, her bottom lip quivering. Was she suppressing a smile? he wondered. No-nonsense, never-cracks-a smile Miller?

"I don't suppose we can put you in a dress," she said, her lip quivering just a bit more.

Dakota raised an eyebrow at her. He supposed the image was funny, but he hadn't pegged the housekeeper as the smart-aleck type. Deciding he liked this side of her, he grinned. "Why not? I've got great legs."

She finally smiled. And when she did, her entire face came alive. "I hope it won't come to that." She reached down and scooped up the dog. "Say hello to her. How you talk to an animal is important."

Okay, now he felt stupid. Sugar, her gold hair bow angled

like a crown, looked like the queen bee in Mrs. Miller's arms, just waiting for him to make an ass out of himself.

"Hi, Sugar," he said.

The dog turned her white fluffy head away, and Mrs. Miller snorted. "Your voice is too deep."

Dakota frowned, wondering what in the hell he had gotten himself into. "It's called testosterone. I can't help it." Hadn't they already discussed the fact that he was a man?

"Of course you can help it," she scolded. "Haven't you ever talked to a baby?"

A baby? "Actually, no." His lifestyle didn't lend itself to pink and blue bundles. Dakota didn't know diddly about kids, especially the diaper-clad variety.

Mrs. Miller tsked, and he wondered if she had given up on him. She placed the Maltese on the floor, then asked, "So what have you been doing to get Sugar's attention?"

He reached into his pocket and produced the doggie treats. The older woman made another disapproving noise. "I think we can do better than that."

"Better than that" turned out to be pan-fried bits of filet mignon. "Grandma's making you something special," Mrs. Miller told Sugar, who sat sniffing the air.

Grandma? Dakota shook his head. He sure as hell hoped that didn't make him the dog's—

"Daddy's going to help," the gray-haired lady added, shooting him a you-better-get-involved glance. "Aren't you, Lieutenant?"

Daddy seasoned the steak, thinking he'd just lost his mind. All this fuss for a five-pound mutt.

They waited for the meat to cool. Sugar let out a few anxious yips, wiggling impatiently on the floor. Dakota didn't make a move without Mrs. Miller's instruction. The housekeeper had taken charge, giving orders the way his mother sometimes did, outranking him with feminine skill.

"Now you can feed her," she told him. "One piece at a time."

He knelt and offered the treat. As badly as Sugar wanted

the steak, she didn't forget herself. She looked up at Mrs. Miller and whined, clearly pleading for help.

"Go on," the older lady urged. "He won't hurt you."

The dog inched closer and took the meat. Dakota grinned, feeling like he'd just scaled a mountain. He continued hand feeding Sugar, and by the time she'd devoured the last piece, the pooch was sitting on his lap.

Mrs. Miller smiled. "You realize we've just spoiled her for life?"

"It's for an important cause."

"I know," the woman said gently. "It would be nice if Kathy and Sugar moved in permanently. I like your wife, Lieutenant. You're good for each other."

"Thank you." His heart went soft. "I think so, too."

On Saturday morning, Kathy woke with the sun. It was too early to get ready for the carnival, so she brushed her teeth and slipped on her chenille robe, preparing to start a pot of coffee.

Sugar roused from her spot on the bed and followed Kathy into the hall. But as they passed Dakota's room, the dog nudged open the crack in the door.

"Sugar, no!" Kathy's warning came too late. The Maltese had already darted inside.

Without a second thought, Kathy went after her, then stopped when she neared the bed. Dakota was still asleep, the sheets tangled around his waist, the quilt kicked away from him. His face, she noticed, was dark and angular, the tiny lines around his eyes prominent in the morning light. Black hair spiked against his pillow, and beard stubble shadowed his jaw.

He looked warm and touchable, she thought. Like the man she had married, yet slightly changed. She wanted to tame his hair, skim his cheek. But she knew better. He wasn't hers anymore. Too much time had passed, too much heartache. And he was still a soldier. Soon there would be another mission. Dakota wouldn't remain idle for long.

So why was she here, standing in his room, longing for

what could never be? What had possessed her to get this close to him?

Good grief. Sugar. One long, stolen glance at Dakota and she had forgotten about the dog.

"Sugar," she whispered, looking around the room. "Come on, sweetie, we have to go."

A movement from the bed caught her eye, and a familiar being emerged from beneath the rumpled quilt—two black eyes, a mass of silky white fur and a half-cocked metallic bow.

Kathy sent the dog a scolding glance, keeping her voice hushed. "What are you doing in his bed? You don't even like him."

As if determined to defy Kathy's words, Sugar picked her way around the tangled sheets and settled herself right next to Dakota, snug against his bare chest.

Kathy had to smile. The big man and the little dog were an odd, but tender sight. Sugar's white paw rested on Dakota's arm, and he nuzzled closer, stirring in his sleep.

She turned to leave them alone, but only got as far as the door.

"Kathy?"

She turned back to see Dakota squinting at her. She should have known he would awaken. Dakota was a light sleeper. She assumed it came from his military background, night after night of sleepless combat. "I'm sorry I disturbed you. I was looking for Sugar."

"She's right here. Did I oversleep?"

"No. It's still early."

He sent her a boyish smile. "Wanna join us?"

She did. God help her, she did. "No. I'm already up. I think I'll just go start a pot of coffee. Maybe fix an omelet."

He glanced down at the dog, then straightened her bow in what seemed like a paternal gesture. Kathy steadied herself. The image in her head made her knees weak—Dakota with the child they should have had—a dark-eyed, dark-haired little girl dressed in ruffles and ribbons.

"Sweetheart?"

"Yes?" She responded to the endearment, hating that it made her weaker, more vulnerable, achy inside.

"If you give me a few minutes, I'll help you with breakfast."

"Just meet me in the kitchen when you're ready." She forced her legs to carry her down the hall, wondering how she was going to survive the carnival—an event overflowing with dark-eyed, dark-haired children.

Kathy started the coffee and by the time the hash browns were cooking, Dakota arrived with Sugar in tow. He had showered, shaved and zipped himself into a pair of jeans.

He made his way around her, the Maltese at his heels. Kathy couldn't help but wonder what had turned Sugar around. Had the dog looked at him this morning and decided he was just too gorgeous to ignore?

They fixed breakfast and sat across from each other at the dining-room table, their plates filled with potatoes and eggs.

"So, have you found a house yet?" he asked.

Kathy shook her head. "No." None of the rentals seemed quite right. They were all too big for one person, too spacious and lonely. She wanted charming and cozy, like the cottage in Asterland. Or a place that would make her feel warm and woodsy, like Dakota's ranch. She needed the perfect, permanent home, something her living-abroad parents had never provided.

"What about office space?" he asked, pursuing their conversation.

"I haven't looked." She had been too busy scouting Royal for a house that probably didn't exist. "But I guess I'd better start. My parents are anxious for me to get this location up and running."

He lifted his coffee. "Do they know you're staying with me?"

"Yes." And they approved. They didn't understand why Kathy had left Dakota in the first place. One lost baby, her mother had told her, didn't mean that she couldn't have another. And Dakota had been a soldier when she'd married him, so walking out on him two years later made no sense.

Kathy's pragmatic parents didn't understand the dreamer in her, the old-fashioned girl who wanted an enchanted garden, a house full of children and a husband who cared more about saving his marriage than saving the world.

Hiding a frown, she sipped her juice. Her mother had been the first to suggest Royal as a satellite location. That didn't mean her parents were playing matchmaker, did it? Her proper, professional, business-minded parents? No. That couldn't be.

A small, whining noise jarred Kathy from her thoughts. "Is that Sugar?" She looked around to see the dog sitting at Dakota's feet. "Is she begging?"

"No," he answered hastily. "She's just watching me eat."

Watching him eat? "You've been feeding her table scraps, haven't you?" No wonder Sugar followed him around like a lovesick fool. It was food she was after, not masculine attention.

Dakota winced. "Maybe I've given her a few bites here and there. But it wasn't my idea. Mrs. Miller put me up to it."

His boyish excuse sounded impossibly endearing. "And why would your housekeeper do that?"

"Because I asked her to help me make friends with your dog."

A burst of moisture rushed behind Kathy's eyes. She blinked, refusing to cry over breakfast. It had to be, she thought, the sweetest, silliest thing he had ever done. She smiled and reached across the table for his hand. "Sometimes you surprise me."

His fingers curled around hers. "You surprise me, too."

Sugar leapt onto Dakota's lap, and Kathy laughed. Suddenly she was looking forward to spending the day with her husband, even in the company of dark-eyed, dark-haired children.

Beneath the Texas sun, a small park in Midland had been transformed into a carnival, its grassy spaces filled with merriment. It wasn't a large affair, not the kind with those whip-

lash-type rides, but it was entertaining nonetheless. It reminded Dakota of being a kid himself, of the Halloween
festival his elementary school used to host every October. His
mother had been involved in that, too. Dakota figured being
on the board of directors at the Indian Center was a lot like
being a PTA mom for Violet Tenewa. Only these days, she
had more than one child to look after. She had taken on a
caseload of foster kids.

Dakota sniffed the air, the aroma of hot dogs and buttered
popcorn teasing his senses. Kathy had been placed in one of
the concession stands, and he could see her from his post at
the shooting gallery. She wore slim-fitting jeans and a buck-
skin-colored T-shirt, a thick ponytail bouncing high on her
head. She seemed right at home, filling cartons of popcorn
and handing out candy apples.

Looking up from a customer, she noticed him watching her,
then graced him with a quick, ladylike smile.

He returned the smile, feeling like a tall, love-struck adolescent, a Comanche youth just coming into his own.

They lost eye contact over the crowd, and Dakota glanced
back at the prizes lined on the shelves—the stuffed animals
and plastic toys. Suddenly he wished Kathy had been a part
of his early years. Maybe if they had been childhood sweet-
hearts, their lives would have been too connected for her to
sever the tie as she had.

A middle-aged man placed a stack of tickets on the counter.
"For the boys," he said, a friendly smile working its way
across his face.

Dakota took the tickets and scanned "the boys." Three of
them, each a different shade of brown. Foster kids, he
thought, and a fair-skinned foster dad who believed in rain-
bows. It made him like the man, respect him for doing something Dakota would have never considered. Kids, no matter
what their shape or hue, were foreign to Dakota.

"You're Violet's son, right?" the foster dad asked, as each
boy claimed a rifle and studied the ducks moving across the
target.

Nodding, he extended his hand. "Dakota Lewis."

The other man gave a hearty shake. "Bob Calhoun." He motioned to the child at the end of the row, his voice suddenly quiet. "That one's Jake. He's Comanche. Violet said I ought to mention that. You know, since Jake's in the program."

In other words, Dakota thought, Jake was in need of an Indian mentor. A Comanche, he supposed, wondering if his mom was lurking somewhere, watching his befuddled expression.

What did he know about being a mentor? Jake appeared to be about five, with thick brown hair and skin about the same color as Dakota's. A mixed-blood, he surmised, like himself.

The boy wiggled as he fired at the ducks, even though his tongue darted out in a gesture defining serious concentration. Dakota figured all kids that age were squirmy and active. No, he wouldn't know what to say or do with someone that small.

The tallest of Bob's boys earned himself a prize. Dakota let him pick through the toys, his foster brothers crowding him in excitement as he chose a plastic snake. He looked up at Dakota with a ready smile. "I'm Scott. Me and him are Cherokee," he said, nudging the boy on his left. "Just like Bob's stepdad."

So Bob had been raised in an Indian home. Somehow that made sense. The rainbow was a part of his upbringing. Dakota assumed Bob's stepfather was a mentor to the two Cherokee boys.

"Nice to meet you guys, I'm Dakota. I'm from the Comanche Nation."

"Cool." Scott put his arm around the third child. "So is Jake."

At the mention of his name, Jake flashed a gap-filled grin. He was the littlest of the bunch and the most wiggly. Dakota resisted the urge to smooth his hair. For an instant, Jake reminded him of Prince Eric.

The kids went back to their rifles, and Dakota returned to Bob.

"You know, Jake has a twin sister," Bob said. "Pretty girl named Jenny. She lives with us, too." He motioned toward another booth and chuckled. "She's with my wife. Those two are determined to bring home a goldfish."

Twins. He could only assume Jake and Jenny were a package deal. A boy and a girl who needed a Comanche mentor, someone who could help them stay connected to their roots. It made him wonder how they had ended up in foster care in the first place. Were they orphaned? Abused? Neglected?

When their tickets ran out, Bob and his lively brood said goodbye and headed in the direction of the goldfish toss, Dakota staring after them.

Fifteen minutes later, Violet arrived with Dakota's replacement. Rather than accuse his mother of setting him up, he strolled the carnival grounds with her, waiting for Kathy's shift to end.

"Tell me about them, Mom."

"Jake and Jenny?" She took his arm as they passed a vendor selling Texas trinkets. "Their father is Comanche, but he's been out of the picture for quite a while. And their mother is in rehab for drug abuse." When Dakota frowned, Violet squeezed his arm. "She's not a bad person, she just got caught up in something bad. She loves her kids, and she's working hard to stay clean."

"That's good."

"Jake and Jenny are perfect for the mentor program. They're doing well at Bob's, but he isn't familiar with Comanche practices." She stopped to gaze up at him. "They're sweet kids, and they're mixed-bloods, Dakota. Like you."

He let out a breath, confused by his emotions. "You don't have to push so hard. I've already decided to come into the center and find out more about the program. But, Mom—"

"Yes?"

"I can't make any promises."

She kept her eyes on his. "It's enough that you're thinking about it."

Was it? he wondered. Thinking and doing weren't the same thing. He didn't know if he had what it took to make a difference in Jake and Jenny's lives. What if they sensed his uneasiness? His inexperience with kids? And how many Saturdays would he be free to mentor? Thunder had already contacted him about the possibility of another assignment.

Nine

At dusk Kathy and Dakota sat on the lawn, the carnival twinkling around them. Enjoying each other's company, they sipped ice-cold lemonade and ate a variety of junk food.

Kathy savored the sweet, sugary taste of cotton candy melting on her tongue. Her fingers were sticky, but she didn't care. It made her feel young and free, a girl without a care in the world. She hadn't felt that way in a long time. Life had a way of crushing those moments.

Dakota munched on chili dogs dripping with melted cheese. He spilled a glob on his jeans, wiped it with a napkin and grinned.

"Do you ever wish we had known each other when we were kids?" he asked.

Kathy reached for her drink, the question surprising her. Dakota wasn't a dreamer. He didn't try to turn people or places into something they weren't. They had grown up worlds apart, and she assumed he accepted their differences. "I've thought about it." But the fantasy never played out quite right. "Since you're nine years my senior, I don't think we would have been friends."

"I forgot about our age difference." He chuckled. "And here I was picturing myself as your first lover. Sixteen-year-olds parked in an empty field, kissing and groping."

She laughed, too. "When you were sixteen I was seven. And when I was sixteen, you were twenty-five."

After polishing off two chili cheese dogs, he attacked a carton of fries. "So much for that romantic illusion."

Kathy leaned back, wondering what had made him imagine such a thing in the first place. Was it the carnival? The teenagers holding hands and stealing kisses? When dusk arrived, so had the Texas youth—long, lanky boys in cowboy hats and girls with fresh, pretty faces.

"I didn't know kissing and groping in the back of a pickup was romantic," she said, angling her head to study him. He had been long and lean as a youth, too. Or so he appeared in the photographs his mother kept in leather-bound albums. And his first vehicle had been a shiny red Ford, much like the truck he drove today.

"It is to sixteen-year-old boys." Lifting a fry, he dunked it into a plastic cup brimming with ketchup. "And I did my fair share."

"Should I be jealous?" Once the words were out, she could have kicked herself. They might be legally married, but they were no longer a couple. Jealousy didn't fit into the equation.

He didn't appear to notice her blunder. Either that or he was having too much fun reminiscing to care. "You know who drove the boys in Royal wild?" he said wistfully. "Lori Lynn Thorton and her thirty-six-double-Ds."

Kathy found herself amused. He sounded ridiculously male. "Was she your first?"

"In my dreams, maybe." He shoved a fry into his mouth. "Lori's older brother was a body builder. Mr. Universe or something. I swear, the ground rumbled when he walked." Dakota went after another fry. "Hell, Lori's probably still a virgin."

"Yes," Kathy quipped, nudging his foot with her own. "Poor Lori Lynn and her double-Ds. She probably joined a convent. Took a vow of chastity."

He pushed back, his boot against hers. "Yeah, and Mr. Universe probably has love handles and a beer belly by now."

They looked at each other and laughed, their feet still touching. It felt strangely intimate, she thought. Casual and loving.

When their laughter faded, Kathy let the wind caress her face. The air was light and stirring, the noise from the carnival almost dreamy and far away. And the sky, she noticed, was painted with streaks of lavender and soft shades of blue.

She finished her drink and thought about what Dakota had called his romantic illusion. No, he hadn't been her first lover, not in the literal sense, but he had been the first man to awaken her desires. To bring her to a mind-spinning climax, to melt her bones and heat her skin, to leave her dizzy and trembling.

He knew, of course. During a fainthearted moment in Italy, she had told him. And he had reacted with sheer masculine pleasure, pushing his tongue into her mouth and carrying her swiftly to his bed.

She remembered how incredible that moment had been, how smooth and seductive, the mountain air blowing in through an open window, billowing the curtains.

Wondrous love. Deep, possessive strokes. She could still feel him moving between her legs, promising a lifetime of forever. He had asked her to marry him that night, his eyes dark and intense, waiting for an answer.

"Kathy?"

She placed her cup against her forehead, realizing how warm she had become. How suddenly warm. "Yes?"

"Are you okay?"

She blinked and lowered the cup. "What?"

"You seem a little out of it."

"I'm thirsty," she said, as if that should account for her dazed behavior. "My drink is gone."

He handed her his, and she placed her mouth on the straw,

thinking she could taste him there. It was, of course, her imagination, her weakness. The part of her that still fantasized about him, that let herself remember the past.

"I was just thinking about Asterland," he said.

She allowed the lemonade to cool her, then took another slow, steady sip for safe measure. They had made love in Asterland, and that was something she hoped he didn't want to discuss. Not now, not while her body was already wandering in that direction. She couldn't pour the drink over her skin, even if it craved something cold and wet.

"You were?"

He nodded. "I was wondering what you thought of Thunder."

Relief flooded her system. Thunder she could deal with. "I liked him. He was nice."

"Nice?" Dakota made a disbelieving face. "Women don't refer to him as *nice*."

Her senses, thank goodness, were returning. And to prove it to herself, she handed Dakota the lemonade. "Then how do they refer to him?"

"Oh, I don't know. A hunk. A flirt. A womanizer. Something along those lines."

"Well, I thought he was nice. The perfect gentleman."

The look he gave her could have split hairs. "Now I know you're lying."

And now she knew her conversation with Thunder hadn't reached Dakota's ears.

Dakota misses you, Kathy.

He told you that?

No, but I recognize the signs.

"Did you know Thunder was married?" she asked.

Dakota's jaw nearly dropped. "Well if that's the case then he's been cheating big-time. Boy, did he play a number on you. Pretending to be blissfully wed."

She shook her head. Trust a man to jump to that conclusion, especially a man whose father had kept a wife and a mistress. "He's not married now. It was a long time ago."

"So he's divorced?" Dakota asked, his tone quieter.

She nodded. "He didn't say why. Just that things didn't work out." And it was Thunder's wife who had filed the papers, that much Kathy sensed.

Dakota drew his knees up. "I guess I shouldn't have said what I did. But he's never mentioned an ex-wife to me. Then again, we rarely talk about our personal lives."

No, she thought, but they go on missions together, dodging bullets and trying to save the world. How ironic that neither one of them could save something as sacred as a marriage. They were more like brothers than they knew.

"I just spoke to Thunder a few days ago." Dakota collected their empty food containers and shoved them in a bag. "He might need my help."

Kathy's heart slammed against her chest. "With what?" she asked, although she knew. An assignment. An undercover mission. More bullets. More danger.

"Thunder has been tracking the leader of a prominent terrorist band for years. And just recently, he got another lead. Whether or not it will pan out remains to be seen."

She forced out a breath. "So if it pans out, he'll need you."

"Yes, but it will probably be a while. Thunder could be tagging this lead for months. He won't bring me into it until he's certain that he's on the right track."

How could Dakota sound so casual, so relaxed? Didn't he know what news like that did to her?

Of course, he didn't. And he never would. Because even if she told him, it wouldn't matter. She was back in Royal, and Dakota was caught up in another mission.

A knot formed in Kathy's stomach. Soon she would have to contact an attorney about filing for divorce. What other choice did she have?

Dakota Lewis was a soldier, not a husband. Nothing would stop him from pursuing his life's work. Ending their marriage was the only answer. Even is she still loved him.

The weekend wasn't over. The sun rose on Sunday, even if Kathy's heart refused to shine. The decision she had made yesterday left her cold and shaken.

Divorce. The word sounded so final, so permanent—a le-
gality she had been avoiding for three long, hopeful years.
Three years of waiting for Dakota to come to her, to choose
their marriage over his work. But hiding her head in the sand
wasn't going to change the facts. She was back in Royal, and
Dakota hadn't thought twice about getting involved in another
mission. When Thunder needed him, he would go. And she
would be left alone.

Again.

Remembering where she was, Kathy took a deep breath
and told herself to relax. The weather was perfect for a pool-
side barbecue, and Sheikh Rassad had gone to great lengths
to entertain his guests. A buffet table displayed a variety of
side dishes, many from Ben's homeland, including several
large platters of *hummus* and baskets of pita bread. Of course,
the thick prime cuts of beef being seasoned for the grill were
pure Texas.

Kathy studied her host and decided he and his wife were
an unusual, stunning pair. Ben stood tall and lean, a proper
man with copper skin and exotic gray eyes. Jamie, on the
other hand, was petite, blond and as spirited as her smile.

"They make an interesting couple, don't they?"

The comment came from Aaron's wife, Pamela. She sat
next to Kathy, nibbling on a small variety of salads. Pamela
had a quiet charm about her, a former elementary school
teacher with twin dimples and a scatter of freckles.

Kathy smiled at the other woman, thinking her young stu-
dents must have adored her. "Yes, they do."

Pamela reached for her drink. "The food is wonderful. I've
never had some of these dishes before." She pointed to a
bulgur wheat salad on her plate. "This is my favorite."

"It's called tabbouleh." Kathy was familiar with Middle
Eastern food. One of the advantages, she supposed, of being
a world traveler. "It's fairly simple to make. I'm sure Ben's
housekeeper will give you the recipe."

"I'll have to ask her. I'm eating as healthily as I can."

Of course she was, Kathy thought, with a tug of admiration

and a twinge of envy. Pamela was five months' pregnant, her tummy a small mound beneath a light cotton blouse. Aaron would be a father in the fall.

Kathy resisted the urge to place her hand on Pamela's stomach, to feel the flutter of life. She remembered being pregnant all too well—the thrill, the maternal warmth. She knew the stages of prenatal development, the miracle growing and changing in Pamela's womb. The miracle that had once lived in her womb.

Refusing to dwell on her own loss, Kathy pictured Pamela's child instead. Tiny fingernails forming, a strong, steady heartbeat, an active little creature kicking its legs and sucking its thumb.

"Are you hoping for a boy or a girl?" she asked, knowing it must be the universal question posed to a mother-to-be.

"It doesn't matter. A boy who looks like Aaron would be wonderful. But having a daughter would be special, too. All those adorable, frilly little clothes." Pamela placed her hand on her tummy in a natural gesture. "If my doctor requests an ultrasound, we're going to ask the technician not to tell us what the baby is. We like the old-fashioned idea of being surprised."

Kathy nodded in agreement. Waiting and wondering had to be one of the pleasures of expectant parenthood—choosing two sets of names, decorating a nursery with either sex in mind.

Pamela kept her hand on her tummy, even when she turned to glance over her shoulder, drawing Kathy's attention to Aaron and Dakota.

The men stood Stetson to Stetson, each with a bottle of beer in hand. Kathy assumed the party was for the Texas Cattleman's Club members who had recovered the Lone Star jewels. It was a close-knit group, and Ben seemed happy to provide a casual, festive afternoon.

Kathy amended her thought as Matt Walker and his fiancée, Lady Helena, headed toward her and Pamela. The party was for the *couples* who had recovered the jewels, those who

shared a common bond. She supposed in that sense, she and
Dakota were a couple, too.

Matt placed Lady Helena's plate on the table and lingered
for a moment, his hand on her shoulder. She looked back at
him with quiet intimacy, and Kathy and Pamela exchanged a
glance, their hearts tugging. Lady Helena was still recovering
from substantial burns, making the use of her left hand nearly
impossible. She also walked with a slight limp, but that didn't
make her any less beautiful in Matt's eyes.

"Ladies." He stepped back and tipped his hat, brushing
his fiancée's cheek before he detoured to the ice chest and
joined Dakota and Aaron.

Lady Helena took her seat and followed his progress. "The
women are sampling the buffet, and the men are drinking
beer." She smiled and placed a napkin on her lap, her move-
ments careful and slow. "I don't suppose they will be interested in food until those steaks are grilled."

"Deep down, they're just cowboys," Pamela said, indicating the masculine show of boots and trophy belts. "Even
the sheikh."

Lady Helena nodded. "That may be true, but he is the only
man keeping his wife exceptionally close by."

"I noticed that, too," Kathy added. But she also noticed
the tender smiles passing between the newly married couple.
The sheikh's young bride all but glowed.

She glanced at her plate, a lump forming in her throat. It
made her long for the days when she and Dakota had first
fallen in love. The romance and passion, the stolen glances
and heartbeats of excitement.

Could she really divorce him? Take that final, devastating
step?

Pamela rose. "I can't resist another helping. Just one more
salad before the main course." She rubbed her protruding
tummy. "And I do have the excuse that I'm eating for two."

As the pregnant woman flashed her dimples and headed for
the buffet, Kathy and Lady Helena laughed. Aaron's wife was
a true delight.

A quiet, reflective moment ensued, and Kathy gazed out at

the scene before her. A Texas-style terrace led to the pool, but an arrangement of pillars and statues resembled the ruins of a classic temple. The sheikh's ranch was a Royal oasis—a unique blend of culture and eclectic architecture. Beyond the pool, an array of colorful blooms charmed the Western landscape with tropical beauty.

"Kathy?"

She met Lady Helena's gaze and realized the other woman had been watching her. "Yes?"

"Thank you so much for what you did. I owe you and Dakota my deepest gratitude, but I don't know how to repay you."

Kathy's eyes misted. Lady Helena was the daughter of an Asterland count, and she had been waiting to return to her homeland to plan her wedding. But the threat of Payune's revolution had kept her from fulfilling that dream. And now that Payune was in jail and her country was safe, Lady Helena and Matt Walker would fly to Asterland to arrange a traditional European ceremony.

"We've already been rewarded by the king," Kathy responded. "And your happiness is gratitude enough. The way Matt feels about you makes it all worthwhile."

"Thank you." The blonde tilted her head. "He is such a wonderful man."

And they deserved a long and happy marriage, Kathy thought. Their union was just beginning—as hers and Dakota's was ending. But she had no right to envy Lady Helena, no right to fixate on the emptiness in her own soul. Today was a celebration, a party of goodwill and cheer.

Pamela returned to the table and the three chatted until a friendly commotion caught their attention. Kathy turned and found herself staring. The last of the guests had arrived. Dr. Justin Webb and his wife Winona apologized for being late, but no one minded their tardiness. Angel, their six-month-old daughter, had just awakened from an overdue nap.

The baby, graced with golden curls and bright blue eyes, clung to her mother with a chubby-cheeked smile. And at that tender moment, Kathy's arms began to ache. She wanted the chance to hold Angel, for as long as the child would allow.

Dakota was having a wonderful time. The steak was thick and juicy, the grilled corn dripping with butter, the beer cold and thirst-quenching. Ten adults gathered at one long table, eating great food and exchanging lively conversation.

He sat next to Kathy, thinking she'd never looked prettier. She wore a breezy spring dress and strappy beige sandals. Her hair fell loose about her shoulders in a shining burst of scarlet waves. He also noticed that she couldn't keep her eyes off the baby.

Little Angel was propped on Winona's lap, waving her hands and making kiddy sounds. And although she had already eaten her own mushy food, that didn't stop her from attacking the contents on her mother's plate.

How did parents do it? he wondered. How did they entertain someone so small? Did they baby-talk and make goofy faces from sunrise to sundown?

"Would you like me to hold her?" Kathy asked Winona. "I've finished my meal."

The other woman removed a squished strawberry from the little girl's hand. "Are you sure you don't mind?"

"No, not at all. I couldn't eat another bite. I've been to the buffet table twice, and you're just getting started."

"In that case, I accept." Winona sent Kathy a grateful smile and came around to their side of the table. Placing her daughter on Kathy's lap, she told the child to be good.

Dakota wondered if that was possible. In spite of Angel's ethereal name, a devilish glint shone in those big blue eyes. Then again, cherubs smiled the way she was smiling, their cheeks pink and chubby.

Her smile widened, and he grinned. She had one tooth, one tiny white chip poking out of her gums.

While Angel bounced on Kathy's lap and laughed, Dakota made one of those ridiculous faces just to amuse her. But when Kathy looked over to see the child's source of entertainment, he stopped acting like an idiot and picked up his corn. Making faces was one thing, getting caught quite another.

Angel laughed again, and he bit into his corn. The cherub seemed pleased that they'd fooled Kathy, even if he hadn't intended to make a game of it.

"What are you giggling about?" Kathy asked the baby.

Me, Dakota wanted to say. He had made Angel laugh. And it felt good, he realized. Babies had never paid much attention to him in the past, but he supposed that was partly his own fault. He wasn't overly animated nor did he have a smooth, soothing voice. He was big and broad and uncertain of how to connect with a being so much smaller than himself.

But he had done all right today. Angel seemed to like him.

Kathy fussed adoringly with the little girl, brushing a curl from her eye, fixing her T-shirt when it rolled up her belly. Angel sported a casual yet lacy outfit, complete with matching socks and a ruffled collar. Sugar and spice, Dakota thought. The description fit the child and his wife. They made a beautiful, feminine picture.

From across the table, Winona and Justin watched, pride glittering in their eyes. Angel was their miracle, a baby who had literally been left on Winona's door step. Dakota couldn't help but wonder how it would feel to save something as precious and tender as a child. At the moment, it seemed far more important than anything he had ever done.

A jolt of unexpected longing constricted his chest. Would a child have made a difference in his marriage?

He glanced at Kathy, and Angel laughed again, catching him off guard. He grinned back at her, but this time his wife turned and trapped his gaze.

"So you're the reason she's been giggling all this time?"

He shrugged, his grin still in place. "I guess she thinks I'm funny looking."

The smile that spread across Kathy's face was as sappy as his, and he thought this had to be the strangest, most heart-warming moment they had ever shared. He felt warm and wooly and kind of stupid inside, but he liked the feeling so he kept smiling, even if a flutter of self-consciousness had crept in.

There probably wasn't a person at the barbecue who hadn't noticed his uncharacteristic behavior.

Angel leaned forward and held out her arms, and Kathy's expression softened. "She wants you to hold her."

His pulse jumped, and something akin to panic shot through his veins. Hold her? Him? The big, brutal soldier? What if he dropped her? Damaged the little imp for life? Or what if she decided he wasn't so entertaining up close? What if she squirmed and cried?

Angel made a loud, impatient noise and waved her dimpled arms, demanding the attention he was afraid to give.

"Okay, now. Don't fuss." He placed his hands around the child's waist, handling her as carefully as a ticking bomb. A feminine temper tantrum would only make matters worse.

Angel came to him readily, no tears, no tiny-female fits. Instead she hugged his neck and snuggled against his shoulder. He looked across the table at Justin, who studied him from beneath a straw Stetson, a father watching his baby girl cuddle in another man's arms.

"She smells good," Dakota said, nuzzling the child.

Justin cocked an eyebrow, a slight quirk to his lips. "Did you think my daughter would smell bad?"

Dakota flashed a chagrinned grin. "No." But he hadn't expected to feel like the sun had chosen to shine exclusively on him. Angel's body was soft and warm, her skin a blend of sweet, comforting scents—powder and lotion and flowers blooming along heaven's pearly gates. He stroked her back, then patted her bottom, the rustle of diaper a curious sound.

Angel wasn't exactly still, but she wasn't a concealed bundle of explosives, either. She toyed with his shirt and moved her head back and forth, her hair tickling his chin.

I want one, he thought, turning to meet Kathy's gaze. A shimmering, misty gaze, he noticed. A woman thinking she wanted one, too.

Was it possible that their sudden fantasy could already be taking shape in Kathy's womb? They had made love in Asterland without protection, and mistakes often produced miracles.

Before Dakota could monopolize Angel's time, the baby decided she wanted to try her luck with Ben. She latched onto the sheikh, and the transfer was made. Ben got a syrupy look on his face, and Dakota laughed. One bright-eyed little girl was turning the Texas Cattleman's Club macho militia to mush.

Within twenty minutes Angel had charmed her way around the table, until Justin claimed her for good. Once she was in her daddy's arms, no other man stood a chance.

After the dishes were cleared, the sheikh's loyal housekeeper appeared with a frothy cake, pastel icing dotted with sugared roses.

Ben nodded to the elderly woman and guided his wife to the head of the table. "We would like to thank all of you for coming to our home," he said. "This is a special time for Jamie and me, and we are proud to announce that—"

"I'm pregnant!" his spontaneous young bride blurted, raising the hem of a pale blue blouse just enough to expose a glimpse of her navel.

The customarily proper Ben laughed and kissed her smartly on the lips, and a blast of excitement followed. The women rushed Jamie with exuberant hugs, and the men clapped Ben on the back and pumped his hand. Even Angel squealed in baby wonder.

Dakota congratulated the beaming couple, then stepped back to absorb the joy, the sheer enchantment of life.

God permitting, he and Kathy would be next.

Ten

Kathy exhaled a ragged breath, her emotions a mass of conflicting energy. Being happy for your friends and sad for yourself presented an uneasy combination. She craved a cup of herbal tea, her Irish grandmother's remedy for relaxation.

"Can I get you anything? Tea? Coffee?" she asked Dakota, slipping off her sandals. Bare feet helped, too. And curling up in an oversize chair.

"No, thanks. I had coffee at Ben's." He removed his hat and hung it on a nearby rack.

She nodded and headed into the kitchen. Searching through the tea bags, she chose a lemon flavor promising to lift her spirits. Tea from the microwave wasn't as soothing as tea from the stove, so she set the water to boil and waited.

She could hear Dakota playing with Sugar, tossing the dog's favorite ball so the Maltese could romp down the hall. The chipper little bark should have snapped her out of this confusing depression, but somehow it only managed to intensify her loss.

Kathy carried the steaming brew into the living room, then frowned when Dakota and Sugar followed. She wasn't up for company or conversation, but she couldn't explain why she needed a few quiet moments of solitude. It would mean alerting Dakota to her mood, something she preferred not to do.

Dakota settled onto the sofa, and Sugar leaped up beside him, a striped ball in her mouth. She dropped it and nudged him, pursuing lapdog attention. He obliged with several gentle strokes. Satisfied, Sugar closed her eyes, one paw guarding the ball.

They made a touching pair, a domestic sight that hurt Kathy's grieving heart. She sipped the lemon tea, praying for the promised lift. Wallowing in self-pity at the expense of someone else's good fortune placed her in a selfish, unhealthy light, even in her own bleak eyes.

She knew better. God help her, she did.

Tucking her feet beneath her, she studied the fireplace. Although the weather wasn't permitting, she imagined burning logs just to calm herself. Winter was her favorite season—mistletoe, evergreens and the woodsy scent of a crackling fire.

"I had a great time. Didn't you?" Dakota asked.

"Yes." But it had been too much for one day. Too many happy couples, too many pregnant women. One moment at the barbecue she had been fine, the next floating through the reverie and wishing Angel was the baby she had lost.

"Are you tired, sweetheart?"

She glanced up from her drink. "Do I look tired?"

"A little. But you look pretty, too."

She wanted to squeeze her eyes shut and make the world go away. How could she look appealing, the woman who wanted to cry because her friends were either getting married or having babies? She didn't deserve pretty.

The tea wasn't working. Kathy's emotions were fighting a losing battle. And contemplating divorce while others found happiness was the self-inflicted culprit. She had spent the past three years pretending divorce wasn't a viable option. At least not to her. If Dakota had made the choice, then she would have told herself that he'd never really loved her, that it had

all been a mistake. But that hadn't happened. No papers were
served, no irreconcilable differences charted. Instead they
stayed in limbo, legally married with no future to speak of.

And wasn't that worse? she asked herself. Worse than no
decision at all?

"You seem happy," she told Dakota. Which, of course,
made her even more sad. There would be someone else in his
life someday. Someone who understood the soldier in him,
who supported his causes. He was too magnetic, too easy to
fall in love with, too attractive to ignore.

"I do feel good," he announced. "But I enjoy casual get-
togethers."

Kathy tilted her head. Maybe he would choose a string of
lovers instead of just one. Sex without serious commitment
worked for plenty of men. And wasn't that the lifestyle he
had leaned toward before their relationship developed? People
did that after divorce, didn't they? Reverted back to their old
ways?

Not everyone, she thought. She couldn't see herself dating
at all, let alone the type who had come before Dakota—Ivy
League heirs who appreciated proper, mundane dinners and
suggested she cut her unruly hair into a more suitable style.

She would rather remain alone and remember the tall, dark-
eyed man waiting for her on the cliffs. Her forbidden lover.
The husband she couldn't keep.

She released a weary sigh. How typical. And tragic. Cast-
ing herself as the heroine in an ill-fated legend—a woman
wandering through life like an aimless shadow, her heart
longing for what could never be.

As Dakota removed his boots and placed them under the
coffee table, Sugar stirred, then settled beside him again.
"Angel sure is a cute little girl." He shook his head in amaze-
ment. "Imagine discovering a baby on your doorstep. Thinking you hear an abandoned kitten, but going outside and finding a child instead."

Because Kathy couldn't bring herself to picture such a confusing yet magical scenario, she responded simply. "Winona
and Justin are wonderful parents."

He sought her gaze. "Yes, they are. In that regard, it was the right doorstep."

And ours was the wrong one, she thought, wishing those dark eyes weren't exploring hers. Why was he watching her so closely? Did he sense her uneasiness?

She set her tea on a nearby table and tried to relax. She didn't want to be found out. Not now, not with the dark cloud of divorce weighing on her mind, with images of Dakota finding other lovers.

"Kathy," he said, still studying her.

It was too late, she realized. He was going to ask why a festive barbecue had made her so sad. She held her breath and waited, wondering what she would say, how she would convince him that she was fine.

"Is there a chance you might be pregnant?"

Oh, God. She gripped the cushioned chair, her heart tackling too many beats. "Why would you—?"

"We didn't use protection in Asterland."

"I'm not." She let out the breath she had been holding, forcing her voice to remain steady. Every cell in her body ached, right along with her pounding heart. "You don't need to worry."

"I wasn't worried. I was actually hoping." He paused to shift his posture, move closer to the edge of the sofa. "I've never really thought about having kids. At least not consciously. And then today it hit me."

Dizziness swept through Kathy, making her legs weak. She untucked them, then placed both feet on the floor, searching for solid ground, for stability she couldn't quite find.

"I'm not pregnant." And his wish, his hope had come much too late. Their baby was gone.

"Are you sure? Did you take one of those drugstore tests?"

"There was no need." She felt as though she were floating outside herself, pushing away pain from the past. Pushing as it drifted toward her, waiting to connect. "I didn't miss my period."

"Oh." He dropped his gaze, then lifted it a second later. "We should have had kids when we had the chance, when things were right between us." Reaching for Sugar, he stroked the dog's sleeping form. "I can't help but think it would have made a difference in our marriage." His smile was a little sad, a little wistful. "You would have made a terrific mother. And I could have learned to be a dad."

Kathy didn't burst into tears. Instead they trailed slowly down her cheeks, one right after the other, burning as they went.

When Dakota leaned forward, she held up her hand to ward him off, to keep him from coming closer. It was time to tell him about the baby, but she couldn't if he touched her.

"Don't," she whispered. "Just give me a minute." A minute for three years of loneliness. It sounded absurd.

Wiping her eyes, she stared at her husband, the man who waited with a concerned expression. The man who suddenly wanted to be a father.

Dakota knew he had said something hurtful. Somehow he had hurt Kathy without meaning to. "Tell me, sweetheart. What's wrong?"

She continued to stare, more through him than at him, her red-rimmed eyes vacant, the sound of her voice distant. "There was a baby. But I miscarried. Three years ago."

"I don't understand." He blinked, struggling to grasp her words. It wasn't something he expected to hear, to comprehend. "Why didn't you tell me when you found out you were pregnant? When…?" He let his next question drift, unable to say it out loud.

"Because you weren't here. Not during any of it." Her voice broke a little, and he knew she forced back another flood of tears, another knot of emotion. "I had no way to reach you. You were on a mission. Gone for months."

And she had lost their child. The baby he had thought about today. The baby they should have had. He tried not to picture her, but his mind's eye refused to listen. He saw her in his head—her tummy swollen, the life inside her flourishing one week, its tiny heartbeat gone the next.

"Did you tell anyone?"

"I was waiting for you." She brushed at her dress, her

fingers curling until they clutched the fabric. "I didn't suspect I was pregnant until weeks after you'd gone. So I waited, hoping you would come home soon."

"But I didn't." And to him, one day of the mission had seemed like the next. It had been a long, grueling ordeal—a dangerous operation that kept him from contacting his wife. "I thought about you, always." But that hardly mattered, he realized. His thoughts hadn't protected Kathy or their child.

She glanced away. "I thought about you, too. Wondered exactly what you were doing, who you were with, if you were safe. I was happy about the baby and worried about you at the same time."

He didn't know how to respond, not through the over-whelming pain and guilt. Was it stress that had caused her to lose their child? "How far along were you?"

"When I miscarried?" Avoiding eye contact, she released an erratic breath. "Almost three months. Eleven weeks. I was just getting over the morning sickness."

Suddenly her answer made it all too real. Too vivid in his mind. He should have returned from his mission to find a healthy, happy, pregnant wife. He should have kissed her tummy, brought her breakfast in bed, shopped for teddy bears, chosen a color for the nursery.

"It happened at home," Kathy said. "In this house. I suppose I should hate staying here, but for some reason I don't. Maybe because I was happy here once."

Dakota prayed she could be happy there again, that they could get through this. He didn't want to lose his wife. Not a second time.

"Were you alone?" he asked.

"Yes. I came home from the market and while I was putting away the groceries, I got this terrible cramp." She clutched her stomach as though still feeling it. Feeling the loss of their child. "I called the doctor right away, but I knew it was too late." Rocking a little, she stared into space, into the memories filling her head. "I didn't buy much at the store. I had this craving for a peanut butter and banana sandwich."

Someone should have been there with her, he thought.

No, not just someone. He should have been there. Her husband.

She kept her hands wrapped around her middle. "I don't even like peanut butter. Not really."

Dakota wished she would look at him, scream and yell, tell him that she hated him. It would be easier to bear than watching her droop like a wilting flower, delicate petals ragged and torn.

"I'm sorry," he whispered. "So sorry."

Finally she turned, "I left this house two weeks later. I couldn't stay here. I couldn't wait for you anymore. I didn't just lose our baby. I lost us."

"I know." He remembered coming home to find her gone, to find himself living with emptiness. "Let me help you get ready for bed. You're exhausted. You should lie down." Dakota rose to his feet. He needed to hold her, and she needed warmth and comfort. Her eyes were still edged with tears. She wasn't through crying. Tonight they would spill from her heart.

She didn't take the hand he offered, so he stepped back, a lump forming in his throat.

"I don't need your help," she said, her voice quiet. "I fell apart a long time ago. I'm not falling apart now."

But she was, he thought. She was barely holding on. She had waited so long to tell him about the baby. Much too long.

She stood and faced him. "We can't change what happened. It's over. It's done. And I don't want to talk about it anymore."

Dakota nodded and let her pass, not knowing what else to do. On silent feet, she walked down the hall toward her room. The day had shifted into night, early evening with an early moon shining through the living-room windows.

After closing the blinds, he left the sleeping dog on the sofa and carried Kathy's cup into the kitchen. Leaning against the sink, he pictured her there, three years before, pregnant with his child.

His child.

Today he had held a baby for the first time—a tiny girl

who smelled sweet and powdery, a girl with fair hair and bright blue eyes.

Pouring the leftover tea down the drain, Dakota watched it disappear. Like Angel, their baby would have been beautiful. It would have inherited his Comanche skin and Kathy's Irish smile—a child whose dark hair would have shimmered in the sun with streaks of auburn.

Dakota sank to the floor, mourning the life he had never got to know—a son or daughter who should have grown into a wondrous little being.

Two hours passed before he glanced up at the clock. While he'd sat on the floor, trapped in emotion, what had Kathy been doing? Battling exhaustion? Hugging her knees to her chest?

Rising, he pulled a hand through his hair. He couldn't leave her alone. Not tonight. They both needed comfort, whether they lay awake or succumbed to sleep.

A pale glow spilled from beneath her bedroom door. He stood, gazing down at the light. It wasn't her bedroom, he corrected, a frown taking root in his brow. It was the room they had decorated for guests. Kathy didn't belong there. She belonged with him.

He didn't think to knock. Opening the door, he slipped inside.

She was awake, wearing the same sleeveless dress, her hair a golden shade of red—a fiery halo enhanced by the illumination of a single amber bulb. Fragility sprinkled over her like a spring rain, each teardrop as delicate as spun glass. Some clung to her lashes, others slid down her cheeks.

How could she look so lost, yet so beautiful?

Their eyes met, but neither spoke. She held a pillow against her stomach while another supported her back, cushioning the headboard. The quilt was rumpled, the sheets only mildly disturbed.

He wanted to carry her to his room, to the bed they once shared, but he doubted she would welcome such a powerful intrusion. If he touched her, it would be with her permission.

He stopped in the center of the room, praying she wouldn't

turn him away. He should have knocked, respected her privacy.

"Can I stay?" he asked. "Can I sit with you?"

She nodded, and he came toward the bed.

"You should try to sleep." He reached for a tissue on the night stand, then settled beside her. Tilting her chin, he dried her tears.

She leaned into him, her head on his shoulder, the scarlet halo vivid against the white background of his shirt. He intended to get her a nightgown, to dress her for bed, but he didn't want to lose the connection. So he held her instead.

Even in the amber light, he saw shadows beneath her eyes, pale lavender circles, swollen from tears. She felt as fragile as she looked, her slim, elegant body draped in a wrinkled dress.

"I should have told you sooner," she said. "I meant to."

"It's okay. None of this is your fault." He lifted the sheet and tucked it around her. Pressing a kiss to her forehead, he felt her breath stir against his neck just as her eyes drifted closed.

And while she slept, he thought about how much he loved her.

Kathy awakened at daybreak and found herself next to Dakota, a printed sheet balled at their feet. They were both dressed in the clothes they had worn yesterday, but his shirt fell open and the top button of his jeans lay undone. His belt was gone, she noticed. Sometime in the middle of the night he had removed it.

He looked rumpled and gorgeous, his jaw shadowed with just a hint of beard stubble. And his hair, as black and coarse as a winter night, spiked against a pillow. The bedding suited him, the wash of Sante Fe colors complementing Indian skin.

Allowing her gaze to roam, she locked onto his hips, onto those unfastened jeans. The waistband of white briefs were barely visible, and a stomach rippling with muscle moved with the inhale and exhale of sleeping breaths.

She glanced away deliberately, but came back a moment

later. Was he aroused? Drifting in and out of naughty dreams? His fly bulged, a masculine rise beneath deep-blue denim.

Palms itchy to touch, she lifted her gaze, and it collided with his.

Blushing wasn't welcome, but her cheeks heated just the same. She had been caught studying his hips, his navel, his sex.

They stared at each other, neither sure what to do or say. She hadn't expected to feel this way, not on the morning after an emotional cry. But last night's tears had vanished with the dark, and now Kathy couldn't think beyond the awkwardness of lust.

He arched a long, sturdy body, stretching a mass of muscle and sinew, and she swallowed, her throat dry as dust.

"Morning," he said, his voice still rough from sleep.

"Hi." Her nipples pebbled against her bra, chafing uncomfortably. "We slept in our clothes." Obvious as her statement was, it was the only coherent sentence that came to mind. Her bra was, after all, part of her clothing.

He grabbed hold of his shirt tail. "Yeah, we did."

Kathy nearly smiled through her nervousness. Apparently he lacked vocal skills on this odd morning, too.

A second later, a heavy breath expanded his impressive chest. She chewed her bottom lip and decided he didn't need to say anything brilliant or compelling.

Even as she told herself having him would be wrong, her rational side refused to obey. She struggled for control and lost.

She needed him. One last time.

"I don't want to talk," she said. Not about important things. That would spoil the moment. The slow, shy heat slipping between them.

"Then we won't. Not now." He moved closer, just enough to send a silk-wrapped shiver down her spine.

"Touch me," she whispered, inviting his caress.

He unbuttoned the front of her dress with infinite care, and the gentleness made her dizzy. The simple white bra and cotton panties weren't designed for seduction, but she saw pleasure shining in his eyes as he discovered them.

Their mouths came together, and they sipped from each other, sunlight spilling like wine. She removed his shirt, then brought her hands to his chest and smoothed her palms over warm, solid flesh. He had the body of a warrior, strong and toned, with a line of dark, silky hair that grew from his navel to his sex.

Kathy reached for his fly, lowered the zipper and smiled when his stomach flexed with a taut quiver.

He kissed her again, this time hard and deep, tongue to luscious tongue. She swayed with sensuality. Dakota was half-naked and fully aroused. As he unhooked her bra, a groan rose from his throat.

"Tell me what you want," he said, trailing a finger down her belly.

Her bra went slack, her breasts aching. "You. I want you."

"Where?"

Battling her next breath, she pressed her thighs together. Suddenly she wanted him there, his mouth and his tongue, but she couldn't bring herself to voice the words.

He nipped her ear. "You said it on the phone that night. I asked what makes you crazy, and you told me."

But he had been miles away in a hotel room, not poised above her, waiting for an answer. "Then you already know."

Removing her bra, he lowered his head and nuzzled her nipples. She slid her hands into his hair and struggled to hold onto the short, spiky strands. He was teasing her, moving slowly down her body, turning heat to hunger, satin to sensation.

"Is this what you want?" He lifted her hips and brushed his mouth over her panties, over the swatch of virginal cotton.

"Yes," she whispered. "Please. Yes."

He complied, pulling her panties down and discarding them. She clutched the sheet and let the fever take control. The blinding heat and cool shivers. The moisture. The edgy need of knowing what came next.

"You taste sweet," he said, opening her fully, licking and sucking, pressing her erotically against his mouth.

Kathy clung to the fever, holding fast and tight, until the stab of his tongue, the deep, wet strokes drove her to a quick and ruthless climax.

In the next spiraling moment, he was naked, nuzzling tenderly. "Do you want me to use protection?"

Barely recovered, she nodded, and he reached for his wallet on the night stand.

"I kept hoping this would happen between us, but I didn't know where or when, so…" His words drifted as he fingered the foil packet. "Are you sure we should use it?"

Her answer came out shaky. "Yes."

"Okay." He lowered his mouth to hers, stealing her breath and the sudden sadness with it.

Now, they both knew, was not the time to talk about babies.

Sheathed in a condom, he entered her, sliding hard and heavy between her legs. She touched his cheek and arched to accept him, thinking how much she loved him. How much she would miss him.

Their eyes met, and they slipped into a smooth, sleek rhythm, watching each other with longing and intensity.

She wrapped her legs around him, and he made a primal sound. She welcomed every sensation, every shiver, every ragged pulse. He kissed the side of her neck, breathed in the fragrance of her hair. She could feel his heart beating against hers, pounding as he withdrew and entered her again, heightening the magic. The pleasure of making love.

Desire swam in her head, like the flow of a long, luxurious current, the water warm and inviting. Touching him, she lingered over the play of muscles, over powerful arms and a stomach tightening with each sexual thrust.

Pressure battered upon need, and the water rose like a tide. Desperate, she took his mouth, kissed him until greed devoured. Him. Her. Both of them together.

They shuddered and strained, arched and bucked, then fell in each other's arms, lovers forbidden once again.

Eleven

Kathy slipped on her robe. She wanted to stay in bed with Dakota all day, but she knew that would only prolong the inevitable. "I have to leave soon."

He wore his briefs and nothing else—nothing but skin as smooth and solid as a bronze statue. "Why? Where are you going?"

"To look at a house."

Dakota frowned and reached for his jeans. "Why can't you stay here with me? This is your home. This is where you belong."

She sat on the edge of the bed while he stood and zipped his Wranglers. Watching him, she tightened the belt on her robe. "No, it isn't. Nothing has changed. You know about the baby, and we made love again. That doesn't solve the turmoil in our lives."

"So we'll make things right." He skimmed her cheek with callused fingers. "We just need some time, that's all."

She blinked, willing herself not to cry. He made it sound

so simple. "I didn't leave because I lost the baby, Dakota. I left because you weren't there when I needed you."

"I know." His voice turned rough with tenderness. "But I'm here now, and we can start over. We can have other children. I love you, Kathy. So damn much."

An arrow lanced her heart, magnifying the ache already there. His claim wasn't enough. The dreamer in her wanted to believe that love healed all wounds, but deep down, she knew better. "You're going on another mission with Thunder."

He sat beside her. "But that could be months from now. Or it might not happen at all."

"What if we decided to stay together and I was pregnant months from now?" Couldn't Dakota see that the cycle would repeat itself?

"Then I wouldn't take the mission. Thunder could get someone else to help him. It doesn't have to be me."

Such easy words to say, she thought. But they wouldn't be easy for him to fulfill. She studied him, this dark-eyed, dark-haired man she had married. He looked every bit the warrior, his face leaner, bones more pronounced. His work suited him, the missions that kept him focused. It was all he had ever known. An honor-roll student at seventeen, he'd graduated from high school early, gone to his parents and told them that he wanted to join the air force. And, recognizing his determination, they'd granted their consent.

Kathy couldn't compete with that, and she would be foolish to try. She had learned her lesson well. "You would go crazy staying home," she told him. "I've seen how restless you get."

"But we're not talking about for the rest of my life—" He paused, then held her gaze, his eyes as dark and cloudy as a foggy night. "Are we?"

She took a breath, let it out slowly. Dakota's panic had already set in. It surfaced in his expression, the muscle working in his jaw, the lines beginning to crease an otherwise smooth forehead.

If only dreams could take the form of reality. She wanted

to keep him forever, live in the fantasy of her choosing. But Dakota was what he was—a soldier who could never be a conventional husband.

"Kathy?" he persisted.

"I can't expect you to change, and it wouldn't be right to ask you to try." She lifted her chin and tried to keep her thoughts calm and logical, her hands folded quietly on her lap. She had fallen apart last night and couldn't bear to let it happen again. "We don't want the same things. We're too different from each other."

He stood, his shoulders broad, his chest bare. He looked big, powerful and combating a myriad of emotion. "Opposites attract. It's what brought us together."

"And what pulled us apart." Her hands fumbled now, looking for something to do. "You wouldn't be content to stay home. You agreed to help Thunder with his mission because that's who you are. A soldier out to save the world."

He rolled his shoulders, the muscles bunching. The movement reminded her of a caged animal fighting its confinement. The battlefield was Dakota's wilderness, she thought, his natural element. And civilization, no matter how much he conformed to it, would always be his cage.

"I was a soldier when you married me."

"I know, but you only had a year left of active duty." She smoothed her tangled hair, hating that she couldn't keep her hands still. "I was eager for you retire. Eager for us to settle down."

"You never told me that. You never said a word."

"I didn't think I had to. I assumed that's what retirement meant to you, too."

He sat beside her again, the bed shifting from his weight. "It scared me a little. Being retired, I mean. I was thirty-seven years old and idle for the first time in my life. I couldn't imagine lounging around in my socks. Or fishing half the day away. Reeling in some poor unsuspecting trout when I could be making a difference somewhere." He turned to look at her. "But I liked the idea of you being home, safe and secure, waiting for me. That part felt right."

And it was the part she couldn't handle. Kathy wanted to pretend this wasn't happening, that their marriage wasn't ending. Yet she wanted to lure him back to bed, back into her arms, into that current of sleek, silky possession. "Sex is the only thing we have in common. It's the only form of communication that works for us."

He glanced at the tumbled sheets. "Is that why you slept with me?"

"No." She brushed his hand, then drew back, the contact too familiar. "I needed to hold you again. To make love with you just one more time."

Breathing shouldn't hurt, but as Dakota inhaled the strawberry-scented air, an overwhelming pain rose in his chest. The room smelled like her, like lotion and shampoo. Why hadn't he noticed that before? He loved her fragrance, her sweet, feminine aroma.

He pulled a hand through his hair. The room smelled a little like sex, too. A hint of the lovemaking they had just shared.

Just one more time.

It couldn't mean anything else. Kathy was leaving him. And this time it would be for good, the final act he had feared all along.

"You're divorcing me, aren't you?"

She clutched the front of her robe, her hand as shaky as her voice. "It's the only thing left to do. The only thing that makes sense. We'll never be able to get on with our lives if we don't end it."

He laughed, a bitter, humorless sound. "And here I thought if we spent enough time together, you would fall in love with me again." His eyes burned, but he knew he wouldn't cry, at least not outwardly. Tears would only humiliate him, and he already felt a sense of emasculation.

"Spending time together makes me hurt," she said. "And I don't need to fall in love with you again because I never stopped loving you."

Her admission should have pleased him, given him a measure of satisfaction, a glimmer of hope, but he couldn't see beyond the despair of divorce. "That makes a hell of a lot of sense."

"Have you ever looked up *love* in the dictionary? Read its various meanings?" Still clutching the robe, she tilted her head. "I have. I know them by heart."

Dakota wasn't in the mood for a collegiate rendition of love. "You know almost every word by heart. In a variety of languages. Why would this one be any different?"

"Because I used to think there were some definitions missing." Kathy steadied her gaze to his. "It doesn't say that love heals. And it doesn't say anything about happily-ever-after, either. But now I understand why those things aren't mentioned."

Because love hadn't healed her broken heart, he realized. And because she had lost faith in happily-ever-after.

Studying her, he frowned. What had happened to his wife? To the woman who relished fairy tales, who dreamed of knights in shining armor and ladies in long, flowing dresses?

I happened to her, he thought. The man who spoiled her fairy tale, who left her alone when she needed him most.

"I still believe in love. Or I want to." He reached for her hand, held it lightly in his. "Can't we start over? Give it one more try? If you don't want me to go on any more missions, I won't. I'll stay here with you instead."

"That won't work." She curled her fingers, her nails grazing his palm. "Eventually you would resent me for clipping your wings. For holding you down when you're desperate to fly."

"You're wrong. I could never resent you." True, he had no idea what staying home would be like. He had never been completely comfortable in a quiet, domestic setting. Making a difference in the world was the only thing he knew, the only true calling he'd ever had. And he used to think that Kathy understood that, loved him for it. But she was right. They didn't communicate well.

Dakota glanced at his rumpled shirt. He had to admit that the idea of giving up his work made him nervous. What would he do with himself? How would he fill his time? And would he lose a part of himself? The man who needed to make a difference?

The questions, the insecurities were boundless. This wasn't something he could have predicted, and it made him disoriented. But if Kathy asked him to stay home, he would. At the moment that didn't appear to be an option. She seemed convinced it was too late.

He linked his fingers through hers, but she tugged her hand away. Not in anger, he thought, but in pain. She was wounded, as fragile as a fledgling with a damaged wing.

She stared straight ahead, her voice quiet. "After I left, I prayed for you to come to me."

And say the words he was saying now, the words that were suddenly too late. How could he blame her for being wary? For not believing in him?

She rose from the bed and headed toward the dresser. "I should get ready to go." She fumbled through the top drawer, gathering fresh undergarments.

She still looked fragile. But the unexpected shyness struck him most of all. They had made love less than an hour before and now she balled a pair of lace panties in her fist as if it embarrassed her to let him see them.

It made him feel like a stranger, a lonely soul aching for familiarity. If she divorced him, this is how it would end. They wouldn't remain friends. There would be nothing left but faded memories.

And then she would meet someone else.

Dakota tensed against the pain, the fear he couldn't dismiss—Kathy finding solace in the arms of another man.

Who would be her next lover? A handsome young politician searching for the perfect partner? Or maybe a widower who already had children, someone who understood her need for family?

She motioned to the connecting bathroom. "I'm going to take a shower now. I don't want to be late for my appointment."

He nodded. Her appointment to look at a rental house. God. How could he lose her? How could he let this happen?

Dakota watched her disappear into the other room, wishing he knew how to save his marriage.

Two days later, Kathy stepped into the kitchen, following the aroma of Colombian coffee.

Mrs. Miller stood at the counter rinsing dishes. She turned and smiled, and Kathy greeted her, surprised by the house-keeper's chipper expression. She could only assume that the older lady's newfound friendship with Dakota was the cause.

Kathy poured herself a cup of coffee and diluted it with hot water, noting the strength had been brewed for Dakota.

"Can I fix you some breakfast?" Mrs. Miller asked.

She added sugar and cream to her cup. "No, thank you. This will do."

"Lieutenant Lewis is in the backyard. He wants to talk to you when you have some time."

"Oh." She looked up, a twinge of nervousness setting in. "All right."

Crossing to the back door, Kathy walked through the court-yard, then stopped when she saw Dakota. He stood, leaning against a shovel, staring at a section of freshly tilled ground. Long and lean in a pair of threadbare jeans and a simple T-shirt, he was a striking sight to behold.

Sugar sniffed around his feet, pawing the earth, her white muzzle dusty with compost.

Kathy moved froward, telling herself to relax. It wasn't easy being around Dakota. Divorce still hovered over them like a murky cloud. "I think my dog is going to need a bath," she said, conjuring an airy voice and a manufactured smile.

He adjusted the shovel. "True, but she's been having a blast out here."

"So I see." Sugar dropped a stone into a hole she had dug and proceeded to bury it. She reminded Kathy of a mischie-vous little girl playing in her Sunday best. A fancy gold bow and a heap of rich soil presented an amusing combination.

They didn't speak for a few minutes. Instead they watched

the dog, the sun shining brighter than usual. It was, Kathy thought, a beautiful day to be outdoors. It almost chased that cloud away, making her forget the turmoil in her life.

"When did you take up gardening?" she asked, breaking the silence.

He grinned a bit boyishly, a white flash against tanned skin. "This morning."

As her heart forgot its natural beat, she glanced away from that devastating smile and studied the trays of potted herbs. Gardens were her weakness, even though she had never attempted to start one herself.

"I've always been fascinated by herbs," he said. "Their healing and cooking properties. But I never asked my gardeners to plant them because it's something I wanted to do myself."

She didn't need to ask why he had chosen to pursue this task. He was home and feeling idle, needing to fill his time, the restlessness that normally left him eager for another mission.

Maybe he had the right idea. Kathy itched to dig in the dirt, to lose herself in manual labor, as well. Dakota wasn't the only restless soul. "Mrs. Miller said you wanted to talk to me."

He nodded. "Thunder called earlier."

"He did?" She looked up at the sky, focused on the vast, dream-like serenity before allowing the harshness of reality to overwhelm her. "About the mission?"

"Yes. He still doesn't know if it's going to happen or not, but he should have more information in a few weeks." Dakota implored her to meet his gaze. Beneath the brim of a tan cowboy hat, his eyes sought hers. "I told him I wasn't sure if I was available. That he may want to consider contacting someone else."

Her mouth suddenly dry, Kathy swallowed. "Do you want to be available?"

"Not if you would prefer I stay here."

"This should be about what you want, Dakota. The decision has to be yours." Reaching up, she secured a bobby pin.

Her topknot was loosening, spilling errant strands of hair. It made her feel messy and disorganized, not in control.

"I'm confused," he admitted. "I love you desperately, and I want to stay married and raise a family. But I'm having trouble making a conscious choice to give up my work. If you ask me to, I will. Right now, that's the best I can do."

"I appreciate your honesty. But I don't want to be responsible for forcing you to stay home." In time it would destroy him, and she couldn't live with the emotional destruction it would cause. Neither could she live with the nature of his work, no matter how desperately they loved each other. "It looks like we're at a crossroad."

"I suppose," he said, his expression grim. "How about if we take a couple weeks to think about it? Don't make any decisions until then. You won't move out or file any papers, and I'll take some time to deal with everything that's happened." He paused to study her. "You haven't found a house yet, have you?"

"No." And what he proposed seemed logical. A few weeks of reflection would give them the opportunity to prepare for what lay ahead. The calm, she thought, before the storm. "I did lease an office, though. Not far from the Royal Diner."

He managed a smile. "I guess you won't go hungry at lunchtime." The smile faded, and he adjusted his hat. "Will you give it a couple of weeks, Kathy?"

"Yes." She fixed her hair again, nearly jabbing a bobby pin into her scalp.

"Good." He leaned the shovel against a shiny red wheelbarrow, but it slid to the ground with a thump. Sugar barked at it, then went about scattering dirt.

The dog's busy paws were the only movement. Dakota and Kathy both stood silently, nearly frozen like statues. It reminded Kathy of the recess bell at one of the elementary schools she had attended. She couldn't recall which school exactly, but she remembered that her playmates used to freeze in silly positions when the bell rang. Kathy, of course, never acted foolishly. She always stood with impeccable posture, her hands at her sides.

"So you're ready to set up shop?"

She blinked, only hearing a portion of his question. "I'm sorry. What?"

"Your office. Are you anxious to get things going?"

She shook away the recess-bell memory, wondering if she had been a dull child, too mature for her own good. "Yes, I'm looking forward to it."

"So what is it you'll be doing? We haven't talked about it. Other than it will be a satellite office your folks asked you to head up."

"I'll be managing the export operations for domestic companies my parents are affiliated with. Besides hiring distributors and reps, I'll be in charge of advertising, marketing and promotions. There's plenty to do."

"Sounds like you'll need help."

She nodded. "As soon as I get the office set up, I'll be interviewing for a secretary and an assistant."

"Well, I'm glad you found a convenient location."

"Me, too."

A hush fell over them again, the kind of silence that had them staring at each other in discomfort. She fussed with her hair for something to do, and he dug his work boots into the soil.

How could she divorce him? she wondered. Sever their tie completely? Then how could she not? He was willing to give up his work for her, but it wasn't what he truly wanted to do. And she hadn't anticipated a complication like that. In her dreams, Dakota never regretted the decision. He was eager to leave the danger behind.

But those were glorified fantasies, she reminded herself. This was reality. Kathy looked away from Dakota. In two weeks they would discuss their decisions. *Two weeks.* What could possibly change in such a short amount of time, other than Thunder's details about Dakota's next mission?

"I guess I better get these planted," he said, indicating the trays of potted herbs.

Kathy should have nodded her head and used this moment to escape, but suddenly she didn't want to. She wanted to lift the plants to her nose and inhale each sweet, earthly fragrance.

"Do you need some help?" she heard herself ask.

"I—" He paused to look at her, move his gaze from the top of her head to the tips of her Italian shoes. "In those clothes?"

She lifted her chin under the tight scrutiny. "I'm wearing jeans." And a white cotton blouse with a lace collar. And butter-soft leather flats sporting a designer label. She should have said that she intended to change, but that seemed dull and proper, like a child who didn't have enough spunk to make the freeze bell enjoyable. "Yes, in these clothes. My blouse can be laundered." She slipped off her shoes and stood in her bare feet. "And I like the feel of dirt between my toes."

He arched a black brow. "More like mud since we're going to be watering these plants."

She shrugged. "That's okay."

"All right." He didn't smile, but he sounded amused. "Then let's get to it."

Sugar, her nose and paws still covered in compost, sent Kathy a doggie grin when Dakota turned his back to retrieve the plants. Surging with excitement, she patted the dusty Maltese. Her first gardening experience. She felt like an eager virgin.

Dakota set the trays near their work area. "I hope you know more about this than I do."

She placed her shoes out of the line of fire. "That depends on how much you know."

"Gee, I'm so glad you offered to help," he said, his voice tinged with pleasant sarcasm. "Now I know we're going to kill every last one of these. By tomorrow morning they'll be needing a decent burial."

"We'll do no such thing." She lifted a plant she thought was dill, then checked the label with a smug expression.

"They're going to be healthy and happy. We'll even talk to them if we have to."

Dakota shook his head. "If you say so."

"I do." She sniffed the dill. "This one makes a fabulous dip."

"It's good for an upset stomach, too," he added. "My mom used to make a tea out of it with white wine."

"See." Kathy smiled and placed the pot back on the tray. "We know more than we think we do."

"A barefoot woman, a dirty dog and three bags of compost." He handed her a pair of work gloves and grinned. "What more could a man want?"

"Nothing, Lieutenant Lewis." She grabbed the gloves and stole his hat, her heart tagging longingly after his. "At the moment you've got it all."

Twelve

Dakota was nervous. He hated to admit it, but it was true. Kathy had promised to be home by 1500 hours. And he sure as hell hoped she was on time. This afternoon, patience wasn't his strongest virtue.

Jake and Jenny were due to arrive at 1530. This would be their first unchaperoned visit with Dakota. Seven-year-old twins. What in God's name had he gotten himself into? What did he know about mentoring second graders?

He checked his watch and cursed. He couldn't do this without Kathy, at least not today.

Striding into the kitchen, he removed a half gallon of milk and considered taking a swig from the carton. It used to burn his mom when he did that during his teenage years. But what good would it do to defy her in his own house? She wasn't even there.

He retrieved a glass and shook his head. Great. Now he was punishing his mom for nudging him into the mentor program. He poured the milk and swallowed it in one long, thirsty gulp.

A feminine sound rapped his attention. He cocked his head. The sexy snap of high heels on the entryway. Dakota left his glass on the counter and followed the clicking noise.

Catching sight of Kathy, he stopped. A cream-colored jacket nipped her waist and a matching skirt exposed long, slender legs. Suddenly aroused, he glanced at her feet, not surprised that she made a pair of professional-looking pumps sound wicked.

He moistened his lips, and she adjusted the briefcase in her right hand. How many of these silent, hungry moments would he be forced to endure? Dakota couldn't think of a damn thing to say. In fact, he couldn't think at all, not beyond the visceral emotion of wanting her.

Almost a week had passed since their agreement, six days of torture. Neither seemed any closer to a solution. He wanted her to remain his wife; she wanted him to be content giving up his work.

"I did my best to get here on time," she said.

Dakota's mind stumbled for a moment, then kicked into gear. The kids. She had come home to help him mentor. "I appreciate it. How was your day?"

"Fine. I'm still interviewing." She placed her briefcase on a small antique table in the foyer. "How are you doing?"

"Okay."

"Are you sure? You seem tense."

He pulled a hand through his hair. "I'm a little nervous about this, I guess. You know, having the twins here." It was, he supposed, the center of his anxiety this afternoon. That and wanting his wife. Missing her. Praying she wouldn't divorce him.

She stepped closer. "You shouldn't be. You've already spent time with Jake and Jenny."

"At their house, with Bob, his wife and the social worker present. Somehow, this doesn't feel the same."

"But you've been approved for the Mentor Program. That has to mean something."

He wished his misgiving wasn't so obvious. It made him feel inadequate. But he supposed his limited experience with

children spoke for itself. He couldn't pretend that being cer-
tified as a weekend foster parent made him an expert.

"I'm anxious to meet them," she said.

"I'm glad." He needed her today, more than ever.
"They're twins, but they don't seem that much alike. But
there is the boy-girl thing, I suppose." He led Kathy into the
living room. "I'm worried that they're a little small for their
age. When I first saw Jake I thought he was around five. But
he and Jenny are seven."

"Children develop in stages." She gave him a reassuring
smile. "I'm sure they'll catch up."

Dakota worried more for Jake then Jenny. He remembered
some of the smaller boys in school being picked on. But that
wasn't a cross he'd had to bear. The unkindness he'd endured
had come in the form of whispers and unclean looks. Not so
much from kids but from adults. His mom may have been an
active PTA parent, but she had also been sleeping with a
prominent member of the community—a married man.

Kathy glanced at her watch. "I should change."

Dakota nodded. "Slip on a pair of jeans and boots. The
kids are interested in seeing the horses." Which he hoped
would be his saving grace. At Bob's house there had been all
sorts of toys to entertain the twins.

She moved past him, the picture of professional beauty, her
wild hair coiled in a tidy topknot, her designer suit simple yet
elegant.

Sugar roused from her favorite napping spot and followed
Kathy. She stooped to greet the dog, and Dakota tilted his
head. Too bad, he thought, that Kathy hadn't leaned forward.
He would have enjoyed a little more leg, a glimpse of thigh.
Cradling himself between those creamy thighs occupied a
good portion of his thoughts these lonely, troublesome days.

The doorbell pealed. Dakota let out a breath and answered
the summons.

"Hi." He invited Bob and the children into the house. Bob
wore a mail carrier's uniform, signaling the end of a workday.
The kids were dressed for the ranch. Jenny had a dark-haired
doll with her, and Jake had his hands in his pockets. Both

stared up at him with curious faces—wondering, he supposed, how much fun he was going to be.

Dakota smiled, wishing he were more like Bob. The other man had a relaxed, easy manner, an unmistakable dad-like quality.

They chatted in the entryway and, before Dakota knew it, Bob hugged the kids and said goodbye, leaving Dakota on his own.

He guided the twins into the kitchen and offered them a soda. He had asked Mrs. Miller to stock up on kid-type food, so now the cupboards were filled with crackers, chips and snack cakes oozing with gooey filling.

"My wife is getting her boots on," he said. "Soon as she's ready, we'll head out to the barn."

Jake wiggled and hummed while he drank an orange pop, and Dakota was glad the boy hadn't chosen one of the caffeine colas.

Jenny, her dark-brown hair fashioned in two long ponytails, placed her doll on the counter.

Dakota studied the toy. "Hey, she's wearing boots. And fringe, too." The doll appeared to be attired for a Texas hoedown. "What's her name?"

The girl gave him a look that said he had just asked the dumbest of dumb questions. "Barbie," she replied.

And everybody, including Dakota, knew who Barbie was.

Insecurity looming over him, Dakota wondered if he should ply the kids with snacks. Or would that spoil their dinner? Mrs. Miller had suggested hamburgers with a side of macaroni and cheese, then ice cream for dessert.

Kathy entered the kitchen and saved the moment. "Well, hello." She flashed a radiant smile. "I've heard a lot about the two of you."

Five minutes later they walked to the barn. And as Jake bubbled with excitement and Jenny reached for Kathy's hand, Dakota's heart gave a warm, yearning lurch. With a light breeze blowing and spring blooming, he felt a sudden, amazing sense of family.

* * *

Kathy held Jenny's hand, wondering how many times she had dreamed of moments like this. Herself and Dakota enjoying the ranch, dark-eyed, dark-haired children beside them.

Jake, who carried a bag of carrots for the horses, had a charming grin, just crooked enough to make him look mischievous. And Jenny, precocious, ladylike Jenny, was a child beyond her years. They were both delightful, enchanting in their own special way.

Upon entering the barn, Dakota directed them to the first occupied stall. "This is Kathy's mare," he said. "Her name is Serenity."

The horse came forward and poked her head out, pleased by the introduction.

"Can I give her a carrot now?" Jake asked, eager to make friends with Serenity.

Dakota smiled. "Sure. But let me get you something to stand on, then show you how to feed a horse correctly." He found two empty crates and placed them on the barn floor, helping each twin onto one. Next he cautioned both children to keep their hands flat and offer the carrot in their palms. "Otherwise the horse might nip your fingers."

Jake laughed as Serenity took the treat from him, and Jenny held perfectly still watching the animal with curious intensity. "She has spots like a leopard," the girl said.

Dakota glanced at Kathy, and she could see that Jenny's observation impressed him. "That's because Serenity is a leopard Appaloosa. All Appaloosas have spots, but the leopard appy is white with dark spots, kind of like the jungle cat."

Jenny turned toward the next stall. "What kind is this one? It doesn't have any spots."

"Nomad is a quarter horse. He's my personal favorite, the one I ride most of the time." The horse snorted and Dakota stroked its nose.

"Nomad wants a carrot, too," Jenny told Jake, moving her crate so the boy could accommodate the animal. She assumed the role of the older, wiser sibling, even though she had entered the world only minutes before her brother.

Taking a step back, she looked up at Dakota. "You called Serenity a mare. Does that mean she's a girl?"

"Sure does."

"What's a boy horse?"

"Nomad is a gelding."

"Oh." She stood quietly for a moment, pondering his answer. "Then what's a stallion?"

Dakota's head whipped up to catch Kathy's gaze. She smiled and shrugged, amused by his shocked expression. Apparently he had no idea how bright and curious a young child could be. He would have to handle this one on his own, she thought. Jenny and Jake were his charges.

He frowned, then let out a heavy breath. Jenny waited patiently for his response, her head cocked.

"A stallion is boy, too."

"So Nomad is a gelding and a stallion?" Jenny prodded, confused by his simple answer.

Dakota swallowed, and Kathy placed her hand on the girl's shoulder, wondering if she should come to Dakota's rescue. The big, tough soldier looked as though he had lost his voice.

"No," he said finally. "Nomad isn't a stallion. He's called a gelding because he—" Dakota paused, possibly rethinking his statement. "He won't ever be a father."

Jenny studied the horse with an expression bordering on pity. "So Serenity and Nomad can't have babies together?"

"That's right. But Serenity could have a foal with a stallion if she wanted to." He appeared to notice Jenny's sympathy for the quarter horse. "And most people ride geldings instead of stallions. So you don't have to feel bad for Nomad. He's not particularly interested in being a dad."

Her worried expression softened. "A foal is a baby horse?"

Dakota nodded, relief bringing a smile to his lips. "You don't miss anything, Jenny. Do you?"

"Neither do I," Jake interjected in typical kid fashion, making sure he didn't lose out on any attention. "Can I ride Nomad, Dakota?"

"Not today, sport. I'd have to give you some lessons, and

I can't do that without making sure it's okay with your social worker first.''

"You can ask our mom, too.'' Jake pushed his bangs out of his eyes. "Mrs. Newberry takes us to see her every other weekend. You can come with us.''

Kathy assumed Mrs. Newberry was the social worker. She glanced at Dakota and waited for him to answer.

"I'll talk to Mrs. Newberry,'' he said. "And we'll let her decide when I can meet your mom. All right?''

"Kathy, too,'' Jake added. "I want Kathy to meet our mom, too.''

Her heart tugged. Being included in something so important to Jake felt wonderful, but it tied her to Dakota in a way that made her sad. Next week they were supposed to discuss their marital status—the choices they needed to make. Choices Kathy was afraid to face. If she asked Dakota to give up his work, he would. But she couldn't see basing their reconciliation on a forced issue, on his desperation and guilt.

She met Dakota's gaze, and he smiled, making her heart hurt even more.

He hoisted Jake up, and the boy laughed. Kathy still had her hand on Jenny's shoulder, the connection easing her a bit. Today was for the children.

"In the old days, one of the first things a Comanche kid learned to do was ride,'' Dakota said. "Both girls and boys were taught to ride with and without a saddle. But the boys had to try harder because they were expected to do tricks.''

"How come?'' Jake asked, interest alive in his dark eyes.

"Because it was part of their training to become warriors. When a boy was young he had to learn to pick up objects from the ground while his horse was running full speed. At first, these were small, light objects.'' Dakota placed Jake back on his feet and continued. "But as the boy grew older, heavier things were used. So by the time he became a man, he was able to rescue an injured warrior. Pick him up from the ground and swing him across his horse.''

"But that must have hurt the guy who was bleeding,'' Jake said, clearly searching for the logic in Dakota's story.

"Maybe, but it was better than leaving him there to be killed by the enemy. And usually two men performed this task together, both lifting the fallen warrior at the same time. There wasn't much else they could do. They didn't have ambulances in those days."

Jenny gazed up at Dakota. "Can you ride like a warrior?"

He smiled at the little girl, then knelt to bring himself to her level. "I've never rescued anyone on horseback, but I can do a few tricks."

Kathy struggled with her next breath. Maybe he had never lifted a fallen comrade onto his horse, but he had spent a good portion of his life flying into enemy territory and rescuing downed airmen who would have otherwise died. And hostages, Kathy thought. How many innocent civilians had he rescued? Dakota Lewis was more than a warrior. To those he had saved, he was a hero.

"Will you ride for us?" Jenny asked. "Show us some tricks."

"Sure."

He winked at the girl, then glanced at Kathy. She managed a shaky smile and told her lovelorn heart to be still. Now wasn't the time to miss him.

Jake and Jenny went home and evening brought moments of reflective silence. Although sadness had edged portions of the day, Kathy couldn't deny how much she had enjoyed watching Dakota with the children.

He would have made a loving, attentive father.

She excused the thought and concentrated on loading the dishwasher instead. She had no business drifting over that emotional line.

Dakota came up behind her. She heard his booted footsteps, smelled the faint note of his cologne blending with the earthy scents of hay and horses.

She turned to look at him, unable to control the attraction rising inside her. The excited flutter. The yearning. The need to hold and touch.

''Would you like to sit outside for a while?'' he asked. ''Maybe have a glass of wine?''

''That sounds nice.'' She dried her hands and released the top button on her blouse, certain fresh air would do her good.

He poured two glasses of zinfandel and offered her one. She accepted the drink, and he opened the backdoor. Wine in hand, she slipped past him, leading the way to the courtyard.

Just as she'd imagined, the air was cool and fresh. She took a seat at the wrought-iron table and tipped her head to the sky. ''It's a beautiful night.'' A vast strip of velvet showcased a glitter of stars, and a three-quarter moon shone with a silvery haze.

Dakota settled across from her, angling his chair so he could stretch his legs. The heel of a boot scraped the courtyard's Spanish tile. ''It was a beautiful day, too.''

Kathy nodded and studied her husband. The illumination from the patio lamps highlighted his eyes and shadowed those arresting cheekbones. She thought his face resembled that of a nineteenth-century warrior, a man marked by a hardened lifestyle, the risks that had become part of his nature. When he lifted his wine, it struck her how delicate the glass seemed in his large, callused hand.

''Children are amazing, aren't they?'' He smiled and rolled his shoulders. ''Active, too.''

She couldn't help but return his smile. Now he looked like a forty-one-year-old warrior uncovering one of the seven wonders of the world. ''You were terrific. Jake and Jenny adore you.''

''Thanks. I couldn't have made it through the day without you, though. I think I would have been overwhelmed.''

''I'm glad I could help.''

How polite they were, she thought. Two people on the verge of ending their marriage, of abandoning the love they still felt. It made no sense, yet it made perfect sense. They cared too much to destroy each other with anger. So they held on by their thumbnails, afraid to let go.

"This must be how parents feel," Dakota said. "You know, after their kids are in bed."

Because her thoughts had strayed in a different direction, it took Kathy a moment to comprehend his words. "You mean the quiet? The close of a busy day?"

"Yeah. I'm tired, but it's a good kind of tired. Rewarding."

In spite of the wine, she vowed to keep a clear head. His admission pleased her, but slipping into a fantasy would only end up shredding her emotions. Jake and Jenny were someone else's children.

They sat quietly after that, both lost in thought. She gazed into the backyard where their herb garden flourished, spilling sweet, harmonious scents into the air. Breathing in that air, she shook her head. The garden wasn't theirs, it was his, along with the rest of the ranch. She had only been borrowing his possessions, stealing into his life. The temporary wife, longing for more.

"Kathy?"

She placed her glass back on the table, wondering if he had read her mind. His tranquil expression had tightened. "Yes?"

"Do you remember me mentioning that Thunder called last week?"

She nodded. It wasn't something she was likely to forget, nor was the fact that Thunder would be calling again, expecting Dakota's final answer. "You discussed his latest mission."

"Among other things." He kept his legs stretched out before him, his boots dark against the clay-colored tile. "I asked Thunder about his marriage. It wasn't any of my business, I suppose, but I asked him anyway."

"And did he tell you?"

"Yes. His wife lost their baby, too."

Kathy couldn't breathe. For one lonely moment all the pain came rushing back. Forcing oxygen into her lungs, she willed herself to sit and listen, to keep her eyes dry and her hands steady.

"It wasn't like our situation, though," Dakota said. "They got married because she was pregnant, so when she miscarried, their relationship ended. He said there was no reason to stay together."

"And do you believe that was all there was to it?" she asked.

"No, but I didn't see the need the press Thunder about it. To me, it was obvious that he had loved her. I could hear it in his voice."

Kathy's hand wasn't as steady as she had hoped, so she avoided lifting her glass. "Did it help? Talking to someone else who has been through it?"

"In a way, yes. And now that I know about Thunder's child, I understand why this mission is so important to him. The terrorist he's been tracking is responsible for opening fire on a group of tourists. One woman was eight months pregnant. And although she pulled through, the baby didn't."

A lump formed in Kathy's throat, but she didn't respond. She dropped her hands to her lap and waited for Dakota to continue, knowing he had more to say.

"I want to be here for you, be the best husband possible." He glanced up at the sky as though drawing emotional strength from the elements. "Yet I want to help Thunder catch this guy. For the baby who didn't survive the shooting. For the baby Thunder's wife lost. And for our baby, the child we should have had."

She kept her hands on her lap, her fingers numb from gripping her jeans. "I'm confused. Are you asking for my permission to go? Or are you asking me to tell you to stay home?"

"Neither. You said the choice has to be mine, and you're right. But I do want you to understand why I'm considering this mission, and why the decision is weighing on me. It isn't giving up my work that scares me. It's giving up the good I can do."

"What about us?" she asked, blinking back tears. "What about our marriage?"

"That's the hardest part." He trapped her gaze, his voice breaking a little. "Because losing you scares me most of all."

Thirteen

———

Dakota walked into the backyard, then stopped when he saw Kathy. She knelt at their garden, mothering the plants. She didn't appear to be aware of his presence, so he remained silent, taking the opportunity to admire her.

Her hair, shimmering in the late-morning sun, cascaded over her shoulders. She sported a blue work shirt tied at her waist and a pair of faded jeans, cuffed at the ankles. Because her feet were bare, he smiled. She really did like the feel of dirt between her toes.

He moved closer, his smile fading as anxiety coiled in the pit of his stomach. His decision-making two weeks were up. And Thunder would be calling for an answer. Soon. Most likely today.

As he approached, his boots made slight indentations in the grass. The garden, small enough to look cozy yet large enough to require stepping stones, thrived just beyond the lawn.

Kathy turned, gazed up at him and shielded her eyes with

her left hand, where the wedding ring he'd given her still sparkled. She hadn't removed it since they'd returned from Asterland.

Why? he wondered. Was she hoping she wouldn't have to? Hoping he would live up to her fantasy and give up his work? The decision that scared him senseless.

"Hi," she said.

He knelt beside her. "How long have you been out here?"

"A while. It's so peaceful."

It was, he thought, as a warm breeze blew the loose strands of her hair. The Texas sun offered warmth and an illusion of safety, something he knew Kathy needed. But it wasn't her own safety she feared for, it was his.

He wanted to brush a strand of hair from her cheek, but he kept his hands still instead, not trusting himself to touch her. Even the lightest caress might lead to a kiss. And that was his illusion of safety. His need.

"Were you talking to our plants?" he asked, knowing she had already watered them hours before. The soil remained slightly damp, just enough to make the ground cool.

"Maybe a little," she admitted. "They looked sort of lonely."

He scanned the herbs. But to him, they didn't look lonesome at all. They grew in pretty clusters, keeping each other company with a variety of shapes and colors. It was Kathy who appeared lonely, she who seemed to long for companionship.

She fingered a sprig of parsley, then drew back. "They're not our plants, Dakota. They're yours."

He frowned, pressure creasing his brow. "That's not true. Everything here belongs to both of us."

She shrugged. "Legally, maybe."

He didn't like the direction their conversation was headed. It sounded like divorce talk, common-law jargon. Rather than continue on the same vein, he said what was in his heart. "I love you, Kathy."

She lifted her gaze to his, her eyes as green as their surroundings. "I love you, too."

Dakota took a deep breath. Such beautiful words. Shouldn't they be enough?

Maybe they were, he thought, at least for the moment. Suddenly the tension eased between them, making the sun feel warmer, the plants smell more fragrant. He picked a grouping of leaves and tucked them behind Kathy's ear, giving in to the need to touch her.

"Peppermint." Before the leaves could slip from her hair, she secured them, brushing Dakota's hand as she did. "It's my favorite."

"I know. Mine, too." The scent was cool yet comforting, as clean and refreshing as a playful kiss on a spring day. It was, he realized, the way being married to Kathy made him feel.

Enraptured. Being with her brought joy and contentment. And so did everything else he wanted to share with her—the ranch, the horses, the newly planted herbs. And the children. Jake and Jenny, who basked in the attention Kathy favored upon them.

"I made sun tea." She pointed to a jar sitting in the center of the yard.

Dakota smiled. It looked like an offering, a gift to the elements, to the beauty of the morning. Strange how something so simple could seem so important. So homey. "Do you think it's ready?"

She nodded. "Are you thirsty?"

For a kiss, he thought, telling her he would love a glass of tea.

"Just give me a few minutes. I'll add some ice and sugar."

"And mint." He plucked more leaves and handed them to her, thinking she looked like an island goddess, with her emerald-colored eyes and bare feet.

"And mint," she repeated.

He watched her walk across the grass and lift the jar. As she proceeded to the house, her hair blew around her like a vibrant curtain, each strand shining beneath the sun.

Dakota studied the garden. They were common herbs, but they fascinated him, made him feel connected to the earth.

Maybe he would take another trip to the nursery and let the kids get involved. He remembered seeing a mint that smelled like chocolate. Jake and Jenny would probably get a kick out of planting that.

Glancing up, he noticed Kathy coming toward him, minus the iced tea he'd been expecting. "Isn't it strong enough?"

She stood for a second, her expression strange, her eyes cloudy. "You have a phone call."

"Oh." He came to his feet, then stopped, reality taking hold. He didn't need to ask who was on the other line. He already knew. It was Thunder, awaiting his answer. The decision Dakota had momentarily forgotten about.

Kathy walked beside Dakota. They entered the house together, neither speaking. She'd known this day would come, and she'd known how it would make her feel. Alone, sad, lost.

Dakota paused in the kitchen and stared at the telephone. "I'll take it in the study," he said. The study was the room Dakota used for personal business.

Kathy nodded, and he lifted his hand and grazed her cheek, his touch gentle. She wanted to lean into him, kiss him, hold him. But she didn't. The phone call wouldn't disappear, and she couldn't pretend it wasn't important, that it didn't symbolize the end of their relationship.

They stared at each other, both silent. Finally he turned away and exited the kitchen, leaving her alone.

Kathy studied the blinking telephone. She stood dead still until the light quit flashing, an indication that Dakota had picked up the line in the other room.

The jar of tea sat on the counter, the freshly picked mint beside it. Returning to her task, she filled a glass pitcher with ice and poured the tea into it. She had to keep herself busy, keep herself from tears.

Kathy added sugar to the drink, then watched it sink to the bottom of the container and crystallize.

How could two people in love be losing each other?

Her heart constricted. Deep down, she knew the answer.

And it shamed her. She hadn't given their marriage a chance, hadn't believed in the power of love.

It was her fault, all of it. She was the one who had left, who had walked out on her husband without an explanation. He had been a soldier when she'd married him, that fact remained. And she had loved him for being strong and caring, for trying to make the world a better place.

But she had left him for the same reason.

Because she had blamed him for the loss of their child. Blamed him for something that was out of his control.

As Kathy stirred the tea with a wooden spoon, ice cubes clinked against the pitcher. Dakota wanted to dedicate his next mission to the baby they had lost. And he wanted to make the world a safer place for future children.

Children he hoped to have with her.

How could she fault him for that? How could she divorce a man with that kind of honor and integrity?

She couldn't. God help her, she couldn't. Dakota's passion for justice was part of his spirit, part of the warrior she had fallen in love with. And she had no right to ask him to be less than what he was. If she had to share him with the world, then she would.

The tea forgotten, Kathy began to pace. How long would Dakota's phone call take? How long before she could look into his eyes and tell him that she wanted to remain his wife, no matter what the cost?

Thirty minutes passed, and Kathy's decisiveness turned to anxiety. What if Dakota no longer trusted her? What if she had ruined their chance at happiness? How could she convince him that she wouldn't run away again, that she would wait for him, mission after mission?

She wasn't sure what to say, what to do to prove herself.

"Kathy?"

She spun around at the sound of her name.

Her heart in her throat, she stared at Dakota. His T-shirt was untucked, his jeans soiled from the garden. He had raked his hands through his hair, leaving the short, ebony strands in disarray. But to her, a more handsome, more noble man didn't exist.

"Yes?" she asked.

"We need to talk."

Kathy came toward him, her limbs shaky. They headed for the living room where Sugar snuggled on a leather recliner. The dog's ears perked when she saw them. Kathy sat on the sofa, and Dakota stood in the center of the room as though gathering his thoughts.

"I told Thunder I'm not taking this mission," he said.

His admission startled her, causing a quick, unexpected gasp. "You can't do that. You can't give up something that's so important to you."

He sat beside her. "Other things are important, too." He turned to face her, his voice quiet. "And I don't want to lose you."

"But you can't do this just for me."

Dakota took her hand. "It isn't just for you. It's for me, too. Something happened over these past few weeks, Kathy. Moments of contentment I hadn't understood until now. I want to wake up everyday with you beside me. And I want to grow beautiful things together. Flowers, babies."

She wanted that, too. She longed to see her tummy swollen with his child, longed to feel the flutter of life. She slipped her fingers through his, grateful for the physical connection. "But what about the terrorist? What about your need to catch him?"

A frown creased his forehead. "It still exists. But saving my marriage is more important. Even Thunder understood."

"I shouldn't have asked you to make that choice." She looked into his eyes and prayed he would accept her words, believe the truth in them. "I want you to take that mission."

He shook his head. "But I can't leave you alone."

She lifted their joined hands. "Yes, you can. And I promise to wait for you. Forever if I have to."

"You're forcing me to go? I decided to stay home, and you're forcing me to go?" A smile tugged at the corner of his lips. "We're quite a confused pair."

Kathy felt like smiling, too. Crying, smiling, holding him inside her heart. "We're in love. I think it goes with the territory. And I'm not forcing you to do anything. But I think we both need closure, and this mission is it."

"Like starting over where we left off?"

She nodded.

"Does that mean we should renew our wedding vows?"

Her breath rushed out her lungs. He trusted her. She could see the depth, the beauty, the emotion in his eyes. "Do you want to?"

He took her in his arms. "What do you think?"

Before she had the chance the answer, he kissed her, his mouth, his tongue brushing hers. Kathy meant to deepen the kiss, but he drew back.

"If I take this mission," he said. "Then it's going to be my last one. Okay?"

He didn't honestly expect her to argue, did he? "If that's what you want."

"It is. There are other ways to make a difference. The world is full of orphaned and abandoned kids. Children who need parents." He gazed into Kathy's eyes. "I hope you're interested in a big family." A grin teased one corner of his lips. "I'm really into this dad thing."

She closed her eyes, then opened them, testing the dream, the perfection of the man she had married. Not only did he want to raise their own babies, he wanted to adopt. He wanted to give his home and his heart to those who needed him. He would still be saving a piece of the world, but this time with love. He couldn't have said anything that would have pleased her more. "A big family is all I've ever wanted."

"Then that's what we'll have."

She pictured the ranch, alive with tiny faces and happy voices. "I think Jake and Jenny will approve."

"I'm glad they've become a part of our lives. But it's even more important that they have a caring mother, someone who's trying hard to win them back."

"You're incredible, Lieutenant Lewis." She stood and held

out her hand, offering him the security of her touch. The warmth of her body. The start of their future.

Dakota accepted her hand, and she led him to her room. There she collected the gold vase the king and queen had given her. She handed it to Dakota, and they proceeded to the master bedroom. Sealing their emotional declaration, he placed her vase beside his, joining the two pieces as one. Next he removed their wedding photograph from his drawer and centered it between two candles.

Lighting the candles, he smiled, anxious to see the fiery glow dance over Kathy's skin. It was daytime and the sun streamed through the windows, but the candles added a touch of magic, an element of quiet romance.

They turned toward each other and began to undress. While he removed his own clothing, he watched her untie the blouse at her waist, slip the faded jeans from her hips. Her bra and panties fluttered to the floor in a wisp of yellow lace. And then she stood naked before him—a seductive angel, her hair falling in tantalizing waves.

They came together in a kiss, her aroused nipples brushing his chest, his hands sliding down her back, over lean, luscious curves. She smelled as fresh as the Texas breeze, like the mint leaves still tucked behind her ear.

"I love you," he said.

"I love you, too." Her voice was breathy, soft and alluring. "Always."

She nuzzled his neck, then slid her mouth down the center of his chest until she dropped to her knees and kissed his navel. His stomach muscles jumped as her hair tickled his skin. He knew what she intended to do, and he had no will to stop her.

She closed her fingers around him, setting the rhythm for her tongue, her mouth. Dakota lowered his head and watched, his blood running through his veins like a warm river. A current of pure need.

Candlelight shimmered in her hair, sending streaks of gold tumbling through the scarlet mass. He tugged a handful, rev-

eled in the texture while she seduced him with slow, intoxicating strokes, her mouth gentle yet greedy.

She kissed her way back up his body, and they tumbled
onto the bed, pulling at the covers as they did. He couldn't
get enough of her. This woman who was his wife, his lover,
the lady of his heart. She had given him the most important
gift of all. She loved him for who he was, for the man life
had made of him. He couldn't ask for anything more.

He licked the tips of her breasts, smiled when her eyes
glittered like emeralds. Beautiful Kathy. She arched as she
reached for him, playful as a kitten, erotic as a cat.

He settled between her thighs, took comfort in being there.

"No protection this time." She slid her hands through his
hair. "I want you inside me, only you."

Dakota touched her cheek. Not using protection might
make her pregnant. He understood her wish, her hope. She
had found healing in their reunion, just as he had. The past
was over, the hurt and the pain gone. Tonight was perfect for
creating a new life.

He entered her, found her warm and willing, wet and inviting.

Together they moved, peppermint leaves and candles scent-
ing the air. He was home, Dakota thought. Wrapped in the
luxury of forever.

Epilogue

Dakota, attired in a buckskin shirt, led a pinto, an exceptional horse he had purchased for this occasion. Pinto horses had been prized by his Indian ancestors for their color and stamina.

Stopping at the fence that separated the courtyard from the path that led to the barn, he waited, the horse patient beside him.

A gathering of guests waited as well, quiet and respectful of the ceremony about to take place.

Kathy's father, Harold, opened the gate and escorted his daughter onto the dirt path. Stunning in a three-piece buckskin dress, she took Dakota's breath away. The beadwork was bright and intricate, the leather heavily fringed. Her hair fell loose about her shoulders, shimmering like fire beneath the Texas sun.

Dakota offered Harold the pinto, a ceremonial gift representing a bride price in the Comanche culture. As the older man guided the horse back to the corral, Kathy came forward and reached for Dakota's hand.

Their eyes met, and they smiled. This was the renewal of their wedding vows. No words were exchanged, but the message was clear. In a modern version of an ancient tradition, Kathy had just accepted Dakota as her husband. It was simple, yet beautiful—a moment neither would ever forget.

A whoop of appreciation sounded from their guests, and Dakota and Kathy turned to the festive commotion.

Dakota scanned the sea of faces and spotted his mom, Kathy's mother and Mrs. Miller, the three looking happy and proud. A beaming Jake and Jenny stood with their full-time foster family, and beside them were the men and women who had participated in the Lone Star jewel mission.

Sheikh Rassad, wearing a kaffiyeh with his traditional robes, held his wife's hand. Dr. Webb and Winona took turns entertaining baby Angel, and Aaron and Pamela caught Dakota's eye and smiled. But the couple who seemed to relish the ceremony most deeply were Matt Walker and Lady Helena. Soon they would be married, too.

Within a heartbeat, hugs and good wishes were granted, along with laughter and handshakes. Angel squealed and flashed Dakota a one-toothed grin. He nuzzled the little girl's cheek and winked at Kathy. Making babies was constantly on their minds.

Dakota escorted his bride to the courtyard where buffet tables of catered food and a tall, white cake awaited. A band had been hired to play soft country ballads—music to sway by.

As the guests filtered into the festively decorated area, Dakota kissed Kathy's hand. The Lone Star jewels mission was over, but he knew the hidden stones still sparkled.

Leadership. Justice. Peace. The secret mantra the Texas Cattleman's Club members had chosen to honor still guided their lives. But so did another word.

Love.

Each man, including Dakota Lewis, had found his one true

love. The woman who would share his home, his soul, his world. The woman who had become the shining gem of his heart.

* * * * *

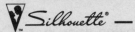

THE FORTUNES OF TEXAS

invite you to meet

THE LOST HEIRS

Silhouette Desire's scintillating
new miniseries, featuring the beloved

FORTUNES OF TEXAS
and six of your favorite authors.

A Most Desirable M.D.—June 2001
by Anne Marie Winston (SD #1371)

The Pregnant Heiress—July 2001
by Eileen Wilks (SD #1378)

Baby of Fortune—August 2001
by Shirley Rogers (SD #1384)

Fortune's Secret Daughter—September 2001
by Barbara McCauley (SD #1390)

Her Boss's Baby—October 2001
by Cathleen Galitz (SD #1396)

Did You Say Twins?!—December 2001
by Maureen Child (SD #1408)

And be sure to watch for *Gifts of Fortune*,
Silhouette's exciting new single title,
on sale November 2001

Don't miss these unforgettable romances…
available at your favorite retail outlet.

Where love comes alive™

Visit Silhouette at www.eHarlequin.com   SDFOT

Desire

January 2001
TALL, DARK & WESTERN
#1339 by Anne Marie Winston

February 2001
THE WAY TO A RANCHER'S HEART
#1345 by Peggy Moreland

March 2001
MILLIONAIRE HUSBAND
#1352 by Leanne Banks
Million-Dollar Men

April 2001
GABRIEL'S GIFT
#1357 by Cait London
Freedom Valley

May 2001
THE TEMPTATION OF
RORY MONAHAN
#1363 by Elizabeth Bevarly

June 2001
A LADY FOR LINCOLN CADE
#1369 by BJ James
Men of Belle Terre

MAN OF THE MONTH

For twenty years Silhouette has been giving
you the ultimate in romantic reads. Come join
the celebration as some of your favorite authors
help celebrate our anniversary with the most
sensual, emotional love stories ever!

Available at your favorite retail outlet.

Silhouette
Where love comes alive™